C000000771

The Antipeople

Sony Labou Tansi

The Antipeople

a novel
translated from the French by
J. A. Underwood

Marion Boyars
London · New York

Published in Great Britain and the United States
in 1988 by Marion Boyars Publishers
24 Lacy Road, London SW15 1NL
26 East 33rd Street, New York, NY 10016

Distributed in the United States by
Kampmann & Co, New York

Distributed in Canada by
Book Center Inc, Montreal

Distributed in Australia by
Wild and Woolley, Glebe, NSW

Originally published in 1983 by
Editions du Seuil, Paris as
L'Anté-peuple

© Editions du Seuil, 1983
© English Translation Marion Boyars Publishers, 1988

All rights reserved.
No part of this publication may be reproduced, stored in a retrieval system or
transmitted in any form or by any means, electronic, mechanical,
photocopying, recording or otherwise except brief extracts for the purposes of
review, without prior permission of the publishers.

Any paperback edition of this book whether published simultaneously with,
or subsequent to, the casebound edition is sold subject to the condition that it
shall not by way of trade be lent, resold, hired out or otherwise disposed of
without the publishers' consent, in any form of binding or cover other than
that in which it was published.

British Library Cataloguing in Publication Data
Tansi, Sony Labou
    The antipeople: a novel.
    I. Title   II. L'anté-peuple. *English*
    843[F]   PQ3989.2.T2/

Library of Congress Cataloging-in-Publication Data
Sony Labou Tansi.

    The antipeople.
    Translation of: L'anté-peuple.
    I. Title.
PQ3989.2.S64A813   1987   843   86-29959

ISBN 0-7145-2845-5

Typeset in Baskerville 11/13pt (Helvetica) by
Ann Buchan (Typesetters), Shepperton
Printed and bound in Great Britain by
Biddles Ltd, Guildford and King's Lynn

To my dead ones . . .
Because to die
Is to dream a different dream.

1

The first time the girl in glasses smiled at him, Dadou took no notice. He remembered only the almost religious way in which everyone addressed him as 'Mr Principal, sir'. The loonies called him 'Citizen Principal', but with the same whiff of piety. He had repaid the smile with a slight tilt of the head in her direction. Subsequently the girl's smile had been repeated three, four, a dozen times. She had even wrapped it in a slight movement of the lips that left Dadou in no doubt. But hell — he was not going to start messing with these loonies of the younger generation. Not that he was especially virtuous. He simply found the idea distasteful. They were just kids, for all their airs. They had had a hundred fellows up them by the time they were twenty. His contempt bordered on nausea.

The rolling haunches flashed their message, and that, damn them, was where the little devils were loveliest. Electrifying. Dadou always looked before he spat. Looked twice before spitting once. But those bodies, flashing their messages — they spelt trouble. Juicy on the eye, but you had to stop at just looking; tiring your eyes out was folly enough.

Dadou had been looking at the girl in glasses for six months. They were nearing the end of the year — fortunately. There would be the holidays. There would be other things, in other places — and he'd forget. All the technology that the devil had concealed in a bodice as dizzying as it was tendentious and that Dadou had caught himself combating, on occasion, with an excess of zeal that put him on edge. . . Then he had persuaded himself that he had a 'right' to look. She offered herself to his looking in a way that always held a snare, at times and in places that always held a snare. Dadou had embarked on a voyage of discovery over that delicious, harmonious, subversive body. He had prospected certain areas, plumbed certain depths, with the hesitancy of a child discovering fire, but only after he had convinced himself that he, Dadou, 'Mr Citizen Principal', was emphatically not in love with a slip of a girl. What sort of a scene was that, a Citizen Principal in love with a kid, if not a big swine being good and swinish?

She had come to his office that morning, still smiling in that selfsame way. Seeing her, Dadou had swiftly but resolutely taken his 'precautions'.

'Good evening,' she said, perching on the edge of his desk.

'Please add "Mr Principal",' Dadou corrected her.

She added nothing. Dadou looked up. Like a radiant body on the point of expiring, she was panting with every pore and her eyes bulged slightly, tormented by the weight of her. . . despair? She was not old enough to be one of the desperate ones. She did not even have their stern expression. Nor their quivering lips.

'You wanted to see me?'

'Yes,' she said simply.

'What about?'

She said nothing. She pulled out the chair and threw herself into it. Her face had burst and the skin, still soft and beautiful, had become savage, bitter-looking. Her eyes were alive — brimming with stars and shadows that made them seem to be in spate amid that sudden drought.

'You don't want to tell me?'

The eyes widened but the lips, dry now, did not part to reveal the usual mouth from which Dadou had drawn, as from a well, a smile of sensual whiteness, a deep, mother-of-pearl whiteness.

'Well, if you don't want to tell me, off you go.'

She stayed. Marking time with her anguish, looking at him almost in a daze. Deliberately, obstinately. Dadou had gone back to writing his report.

When he looked up her face had changed.

'Which class are you in?'

'Fifth-year teacher-training.'

Her voice was tragic. Dadou dropped his gaze.

When he looked up at her again, two bronze grassblades were tattooed on her cheeks.

'Why are you crying?'

'No . . .'

'But you are.'

'I feel better when I cry.'

She got up, threw him a look, and left the room.

The clock struck five. Dadou pressed a button. The door opened and in came his secretary, Miss Sayou.

'Citizen Principal?'

'Is my driver here?'

'Let me go and see for you, Citizen Principal.'

She had shut the door behind her. Dadou felt lonelier than he had ever felt before. He looked up at the large portrait of the President of the Republic that hung on the wall opposite his desk. It occurred to him that it was a good photograph. There were times when he, Dadou, Nitu Dadou, principal of the

North Lemba Teacher-Training College for Girls, had a
curious craving to know what it felt like to be the President.
They stank, of course, such cravings. His very life — or life in
general, all that stuff, that stank too. Putrid, the lot of it. He had
married a young teacher nine years previously because at his
age, in this society that was a hundred times more putrid than
himself, people got married. He had had two children simply
because others before him in this country had had two children
by the time they were thirty-nine. In fact he had left it pretty
late considering that in this country secondary-school students
with two or three children were parents of pupils themselves.
He was principal of a teacher-training college, a graduate of
Kinshasa's Lovanium University — and a former Lumumba
supporter — simply because education was the only branch of
the administration where the stink was less oppressive, the
putrid less putrid, the absurd less absurd, and intellectual life
less of a sham. And also, of course, because others had at his age
or at other ages become principals of teacher-training colleges.
They made him principal of a girls' teacher-training college
because they credited him with a modicum of virtue. As far as
he was concerned, that modicum of virtue was just a step on the
putrid way towards those heights where everything lost its
primal sap.

    And part of what stank, he reflected, was the fact that his
driver was not there.

He got up and looked out of the window. It was almost six. The
girl was still there, leaning against a young eucalyptus tree. The
branches of the tree hid her face. She had the brooding look of
an old oil painting. She was silent almost to a degree to which
no one had ever been silent in his presence — no life, he
thought, had ever been so motionless beneath his gaze,
motionless and beautiful. Again Dadou asked himself: was he,
'Mr Principal, sir', in love? The answer seemed to be no — a

'no' that sprang from every fibre of his being. He was even convinced that such a thing would never happen to him — love, maybe, but not with these bodies belonging to the younger generation. He felt a sudden yearning for an old Tabu Ley disc. He hummed a few bars from it:

Banda yangai bomwana
nazwaka te kaka Nzambe
nako kwamisa.

He had changed the last word in order to situate the song in his own dimension. The poet had talked of 'praying' to God; he hit on the word *kwamisa*. In Kikongo that meant pestering God; it was more human — less putrid, and God must like that. He felt like smiling, but the smile aborted. What had happened to his wretched driver?

One had got into the habit, in that town, of being prepared for anything. As a teacher-training college principal, you did not always have bus-money on you. So you took a 'number eleven' for a journey of several kilometres. That is what we call a man's own two feet: a number eleven, or the oldest means of locomotion. Dadou decided to walk home — a number eleven for you, old man.

The girl was walking ahead of him. She moved with dignity, not like a street-walker. Dadou promptly changed his route for fear people might think he had designs on her. Public opinion was very vigilant here. You had to be on your guard if you wanted to be left in peace; you had to pay special attention to things that did not, on the face of it, call for concern. People had died through neglecting that aspect of life in this city of sun, mud, and tribulations. Not that Dadou was afraid of fate or wished to save face. But how putrid to have the look of a young man, at thirty-nine, trailing around after a girl — however delightful — like a dog.

At the next corner she planted herself in front of him. Without knowing quite why, he stopped.

'Where are you going?' he asked.

'Matongué.'

'That's a long way.'

'Yes — it's a long way.'

'You should have caught the bus.'

'Question of money. . . One can't always afford to.'

'No, one can't.'

They were walking together now. 'When a woman is beautiful and you refuse to find her beautiful — remind your heart to smell a rat.' He had read that somewhere. 'She's not a woman,' he told himself. A child — one of the younger generation, a kid; he felt a strong desire to spit. But she would see — and if she saw, if she guessed, it could lead to complications: she was beautiful, and beautiful women always take their revenge. He told himself once again that this girl must be denied the title of woman, even if she did give off the smells of a real woman. The deep-down smells of a whole, complete woman. Dadou had a weakness for smells — in fact he was over-susceptible to them. It was for the sake of a good strong smell that he liked the occasional chase, and when he had caught his prey he always breathed it in until his nostrils were clogged with it — he felt more of a man that way. He loved that: a man at white heat, distended, exacerbated, no longer aware of anything but the woman and the fire of love.

They walked on. Dadou had provisionally established that the girl was no more than a kid — an attractive kid — and what had started as provisional was gradually becoming definitive. A provisionally definitive conclusion can turn into a definitively provisional one — he was counting on this latter possibility. But the girl's smell was gnawing at his veins, eating into his heart.

'Which way are you going, Citizen Principal?'

Good! Things were back to normal. He smiled at the thought

that the kid had understood her role — that was very good, her calling him 'Citizen Principal' like that.

'Er . . . to Matongué.'

'What's happened to your driver?'

He smiled again. They were really getting into his attributes now. The only thing missing was the whiff of piety that they all put into this beloved 'Citizen Principal'. Also that special flavour of admiration in the voice. But he'd see to all that eventually. There was room for those things — room just waiting to be filled.

'Ah, my dear girl, he's a member of your generation, is my driver — he's gone er . . . picking up girls somewhere in the suburbs. In the state limousine. The public good is a thing of the past here. . .'

'We're all members of this generation,' she said.

'It makes me ashamed.'

'Ashamed and afraid.'

'Yes.'

'More afraid than ashamed?'

'N. . . Yes.'

Dadou recalled the pedagogic principle that forbids blunt contradiction of the child. He was even pleased that the word 'child' should have been thrown up by a body that was beginning to elude his control. In fact 'elude' was going too far — let's say she had sown a certain confusion in the depths of his being.

'Do you never do that — pick up girls?'

He had not expected this question. Consequently he did not have an answer ready. Silence. But silence would be a disastrous answer. He decided to attempt a well said 'no' — the kind of 'no' we are so good at saying: solid, because true. But a bit late, alas!

'No.'

'You're lucky.'

'It's not a matter of luck, it's a matter of conviction.'

'What do you mean, conviction? That would surprise me, Citizen Principal. No one ever entirely convinces himself he doesn't like a bit of skirt. He takes remedial measures. Sometimes they're nasty. Sometimes they're artificial. Sometimes they're . . . *putrid.*'

He remembered that the girls at the college called him 'Mr Putrid' behind his back because of the way he over-used the word. Her choosing it now was an obvious provocation, a piece of almost reckless audacity. Dadou did not like recklessness, especially coming from an attractive kid. He made up his mind to find a strategy that would permit him to conclude a lasting peace with this girl on account of the breadth of her realism — partly, too, by way of a little bow in the direction of her use of his word. She might, after all, have been firing a blank. Dadou fought for composure. How had the she managed to lead the conversation onto such swampy ground? And do it with such facility?

He cleared his throat. 'Obviously there are exceptions — a few. People who in their desire to appear "with it" shun virtue — but virtue exists all right. It hides behind us — and jumps out on us when the time is ripe. People often talk a load of bunk because they think good behaviour is old hat.'

None of the words had any meaning. They had just been something to say.

'That's *putrid.*'

'Who taught you to say that?'

For the first time he became aware that he had been speaking to her as if she were an equal, a grown-up — but he could not go back to the familiar form now without a risk of her reciprocating. Dadou decided to stick with formality.

'To say what?'

'That things are putrid?'

'It's hardly a rare word, do you think?'

'There are levels of meaning at which the commonest word may be regarded as rare.'

'At every level of meaning, "putrid" strikes me as a perfectly ordinary word.'

'What's your name?'

'Yavelde.'

'You're a bright girl.'

'That doesn't do a woman much good. It's wrong what they say. Gullibility is part of a woman's beauty.'

For a long time there was silence. He was unable to quench the word 'woman', with which she had twice lit a fire deep inside him. Their steps rang out on the pavements of the avenues of Limete, deserted at this hour: a mere child, child, child. . .

'Goodbye, Citizen Principal.'

'Are you home?'

'Yes, this is where I live.'

'With the area commissar?'

'He's my uncle — but he's not too hard on me.'

'He's making a mistake. Youngsters like you need watching.'

She laughed. It put him at his ease, her laughing like a whore. She had come close to wrecking his habit of steering clear of young students.

'Don't worry, Citizen Principal — it's none of my uncle's doing that I'm still a virgin at eighteen.'

Dadou walked on. The street was barely lit. There were a few people about. He still had a long way to go — too far for legs that were already beginning to give way. He looked at his watch: nine o'clock — damn that driver — bloody roadhog anyway. Each gritted tooth was a grudge against the man. Making me leg it like a peasant. Sweating, the leather shoes pinching his toes. Bloody world. Groups of market women were crying their wares by Gaby Bridge. The air here was a bit like he remembered breathing on a trip to Harlem — minus the metallic blacks calling the whites blue-faces. But the barbarous odour of refuse, the to-ings and fro-ings, the rows, the shouts, the tugs of sheer life — the whole bloody boiling. Hell is a holy place for us. We worship a hotchpotch. And that tree where they hanged the Whitsun conspirators: after midnight it can be heard singing in a strangely beautiful voice. The bodies can still be seen, swaying in the breeze, and the dogs bark loudly. Dadou thought he could hear the song of the tree: he quickened his pace, cursing the driver for a putrid no-good.

'Tomorrow he'll find out what I'm made of.'

2

Three in the afternoon. The knock at the door might have happened in his heart. Not understanding the feeling, Dadou refused to give any more to it than to an old schoolboy habit. He was thirty-nine, for heaven's sake. And since they had written on his birth certificate 'born around 1929' there was a chance he was in fact older. Or younger. No, he preferred to be older. He wanted — sometimes it was like a craving — to leave the earth in time and in good shape.

The knock came again. Three sharp taps.

'Come in,' he said.

The secretary came in and placed a card in front of him.

He read, half aloud: 'Citizen Nioka Musanar and family beg you to honour with your presence a coming-out-of-mourning ceremony to be held at 81 Bokeyi Street, Matongué, on 15 September, beginning at 4 o'clock. You will be most welcome.'

He looked up. 'I don't know the man. Where did you get this card?'

'A girl handed it to me.'

'What was she like?'

'I didn't notice, Citizen Principal.'

'The least one is entitled to expect from a secretary is that she should notice things.'

'Yes, Citizen Principal.'

He had made the entry in his appointment book and on his desk calendar before he recalled that the area commissar's name was Nioka Musanar. That girl? She had pulled another trick. How was he to put her in her place? How was he to make her see that she was just a youngster, like all the others? She was eighteen. All right, but eighteen was too often seen as some sort of mystic age. Anyway, the uncle must be a bit of an oaf to invite people on the say-so of his niece. At first Dadou thought he would not go. That started the twitch in his lips: staying away would antagonize the commissar — unless he sent a note of apology. He wrote the note. But if he posted it, might it not get lost? The post was apt to be unreliable: it might arrive months late. Saturday was three days away. He would send the driver — no, damn him! He'd think about it and decide accordingly. Not now, at any rate, when he had to send his report in to the political commissar.

This time the driver was not late. In fact he had been waiting for a quarter of an hour. 'Because of Monday's bollocking,' Dadou thought. Bollockings were an excellent remedy. But you had to be careful about frequency and dosage.

'Good evening, Citizen Principal, sir.'

In fact Landu was not wholly of the new generation. Witness his age and his way of combining politeness with politics. He was politicized and polite — not often you found the two qualities in the one individual. Landu said his 'Citizen

Principal, sir' with a note of reverence. In the end, of course, it was as putrid as all the rest. But without his perpetual lateness he might have lived in perfect harmony with his 'Citizen Principal'.

'Good evening, Landu. Wait just a second.'

Everyone knows that with high-ups a second can take weeks, months, years. In this specific case Landu knew the second would not exceed twenty minutes. Unless unavoidably detained, the principal always went home before seven.

The Datsun drew a rope of pale dust behind them. Night was falling — a gift too great for this putrid world. There was a girl walking along in front of them. Dadou recognized her when the state of the road forced them to slow down to a point where she was going faster than the car. She would be walking until nine o'clock. Dadou felt sorry for her. Yet why give a day's heaven to someone with a hundred days' hell? Why teach ten minutes' happiness to a wretch for life?

'Give that girl a lift.'

Landu braked. The girl went on walking. He hooted. She did not turn round. They were going to start looking like those callow youths who went round ravaging girls with the roar of their engines. Dadou was about to say 'Drive on' when Landu bounced the Datsun up level with the girl and gave an ear-splitting blast on the horn. She turned round.

'Get in,' Landu said.

She hesitated. Then, recognizing the driver, she smiled and went to open the back door in order to get in beside the principal. Dadou held on to the door and pointed to the front passenger seat. She threw him a sulky look but, Dadou having pulled the back door shut again, had to get in beside the driver. 'A biddable little tart,' Dadou thought.

The nearness of that dizzying body made the driver shudder. He in army khaki, rather rumpled, with hands as rough as stone. She in purple velvet, with a mass of black hair, severe in its softness, and a radiant face that seemed to be opening the doors of an unknown world to him: the delicate chin, tender, tantalizing, as if encamped there, without fuss — with, topping this strange landscape, eyes breath-takingly whetted, idiotically frivolous. Below, her breasts leapt out at him. She smelled good — a scent heavy with lightness. Like the night, she seemed to light up the car, giving a liquid look to things. A genuine enchantment.

'Good God!' Landu shouted.

A pedestrian had stepped out in front of them. The driver wrenched the wheel round. The enchantment grabbed him and held on tight. Dadou's heart missed a beat.

'Get stuffed, you fucking bastard!' Landu said.

He bellowed insults at the pedestrian but did not stop.

'What street, miss?'

'Bokeyi.'

'In Matonguě'

'Yes.'

'Citizen Principal lives in Kabambala Street. That's not far away. You're in luck. We can drop you at the door. Still, if your parents. . .'

'You'll drop me off first.'

'Yes, Citizen Principal, sir.'

'But this is Women's Rights Year!' the girl protested.

Her protest, however, went unheeded. Dadou did not give a damn about the bright ideas thrown up by the intelligentsia. To him a woman was, to a greater or lesser degree, different from a man. The mutants he dismissed. And if one was so set on looking at history — how many men had been women, how many men had behaved in terms of the women of their day? Women were never a problem but a solution. And then, for heaven's sake, every century had produced not only its poets, its geniuses, and its monsters but also its women — some of them freer than the men.

Dadou entertained these thoughts now purely in order to kill time — of which he had plenty. And in his fear of making too much of the girl he tossed words and phrases into his mind at random. Any words and phrases. There was room. He was plugging his mind to keep the kid out. She might take advantage of the least little vacant space to get in, take up residence, and start laying down the law. The law of girls like that meant complications. He was aware that she gave off a scent of mystery. A mystery that could eventually, if he was not careful, land him in one hell of a mess. How could he, Dadou — Citizen Principal Dadou — be in love? And with whom, in God's name! He ventured to imagine her in his arms. There she was: powerful, electrifying, more full of fight. Dadou thought to blot her out by imagining her on the end of his cock. It was a bad mistake. Because she looked very good there, very much at home, the image capped by the word 'virgin'. That makes a sweet sound, a virgin on the end of your cock, a delicious moaning. He was on the point of imagining her moaning. Dadou cried out: 'No!' — like someone who catches sight of a gun trained on him, with a villain's finger on the trigger.

'Boss?'

Landu, panicking, had braked the car and turned hugely dilated eyes on Dadou.

'What is it, Citizen Principal, sir?'

'Oh, nothing. . . . This story came to me about vampires.'

Landu laughed heartily. Everyone had his old stories. He set the car in motion once more. What were they all, every man and every woman, but boxes stuffed with old stories? The driver was filled with tenderness and joy to know that even he — even his 'Citizen Principal' — was capable of getting a fright like that.

It was no good his pretending he was God — with no needs, no body even, and all musty with principles and calculations. A proper pedant and, as people said of him, the Ten Commandments incarnate. One day, when friends had called

to see him, Landu had heard him say: 'Hang on — I'll be
closing the office in three minutes. We close at five-thirty.' In a
country where people might leave their place of work on any
pretext, however flimsy, Landu found that pretty daft. In fact
while the students called him 'Putrid' the staff had given him
their own nickname: 'the Walking Watch'. They resented his
forcing people to hold so high an opinion of the time. 'The
Walking Watch is out at the moment. The Walking Watch
won't be pleased with you for wasting his time like that.'

They had driven through Limete and the two Yolos — North
Yolo putting on a bit more style than South Yolo. Now they
were coming into Ranquin. Soon they would be in Matongué,
the district celebrated by the country's great singers, where the
girls smelled of sky and water and carried a devastating charge
of sunshine in their loins. Dadou recalled the girl's first name:
Yavelde. He felt like saying it again: Yavelde. Not a bad
combination of sounds. In it he could hear the name of the God
of the Hebrews. A man of thirty-nine could not fall in love with
a kid. Even if the kid did turn into a name filled with mystery
and poetry. Yavelde. He bit his lip. He had spent too much time
thinking about her. He tried to get back to what must constitute
his shell from now on: the word 'kid'. But the word had become
corrupted. It was like mildew. Or like cracks. Mildew grows in
the places one has loved the most; cracks open up where hearts
have alighted. A glance is enough, and the hearts themselves
crack. Kid, kid, kid — Dadou turned a machine-gun on
himself. The word opened wounds in the depths of his being.
He felt sure nothing would ever go deeper than those little holes
surrounded by curled-back flesh. The wind of fear. Fear of
being in love. Oh, if virtue had been the whole problem! Virtue
was putrid. But nature — you can't put nature where you want,
when you want. Nature brings you down. It crushes you. It has
a powerful smell. It goes to your head like wine. Nature can give
you dizzy spells. Dadou let out another 'no' — with less voice
this time, but his whole body felt the shock of it.

'What about a drink?'

'Right. You're a great boss, Citizen Principal, sir. No good being tight-fisted. Got to be loose-fisted.'

Landu felt in the mood for backing his boss into the boldest conversational corners — doubtless because of that 'No!' Not that he was about to be disrespectful — oh, no. Aside from the few times he had taken a bollocking (and deserved it), Landu considered him a very good employer. Not one of those snooty little shits who bombarded you with insults and arrogance and immediately put an equals sign between your monthly salary and you as a person. They reckoned a driver equalled the twelve pebbles he was thrown at the end of the month — and they spent him accordingly, on any old rubbish, or they lost him gambling or used him to buy cigars or beer.

They stopped at Auntie Kamikaze's.

'What'll you have, citizen?' the waiter asked.

'How about . . . one of those great beers from the white countries?'

'Polar? Amstel? Heineken. . .'

'The one before last — that'll do.'

'Citizeness?'

'A tomato juice,' said Yavelde.

'That's not dear enough for a beauty like you. Your body was built to run on super. You don't want to shame the citizen in his *abacost*. That's what the big money wears. (Silence.) All right, what about a nibble?'

'I'll have eggs with ham and banana.'

'Just my juice,' said Yavelde.

'No, no, citizeness. You'll shame this *abacost* here. Won't you try some of our. . .'

'No.'

Dadou had ordered his eighth whisky. He remembered that one did not get drunk in front of young girls. Hide your faults from the children if you would not have them filch them from you. He was aware of the world before him slowly losing definition. Things were assuming strange shapes. He had never been tipsy before. But there, through the general haze, was the kid swimming like a fish in water. More solid, more lovely, moving like a woman. Ah, let her become disgusted with me!

'You'll make yourself drunk, Citizen Principal.'

No — she had not said that. But from just thinking it he had ended up hearing it. He asked for another glass, to disobey the kid. The cheeky little piece. She should mind her own business. A hostess came over and asked him to dance. Dadou climbed onto the dance-floor. He woke up in bed, in a pool of foul-smelling vomit.

He could not even recall when he had eaten fish. And the peanuts? The beans he remembered: that had been lunch in the canteen the day before.

'What a mess — what a putrid mess!'

His wife bawled him out all morning. The children — his two devils, as he called them — had gone to school. Landu came to fetch them at six every morning. The top people's school was a long way off, in Ringhini.

3

It was Saturday, and Dadou had not sent his note to the area commissar. He decided to go. It was putrid when you came down to it, being afraid of a kid. He would go. He was already beginning to see the hand of fate in the whole thing, beginning to arrange for circumstances to get the better of him. In fact they were the only thing that seemed to him less putrid: circumstances. The force of circumstances. It was through a concatenation of circumstances that he had become principal of the most famous teacher-training college in a country where to get on you had to be a cousin or a nephew of someone important. He was the only lesser mortal in his family — in fact in his district — who had managed to climb the steps of the new society as far as the rank of high-school teacher. All his relations were still back in the village, fishing or hunting. They had accepted being of no account in the eyes of our modern ugliness. He thought of his uncle, the healer. There was a lovely fellow!

He treated the mentally ill, and it was generally held that if he could not cure you it was because the devil had got to you first. In the tricky domain of sterility he had even treated whites. Not that Dadou gave a damn about his having treated whites; he had no views on race. But for folk back there the fact carried enormous weight. Whites worshipped no other God but money.

He looked at his watch: eleven o'clock.

'Lola!'

'Yes?'

'Get my *abacost* ready. I'm going to that party.'

That was the kind of relationship he had with his wife. Yet it was none of his doing: they each had their fish to fry, and those they had to fry together they fried together. Dadou had already put his word in: putrid. Habits were putrid. He had loved his wife after a somewhat stingy fashion. He still loved her — her body, full of curves and contours to be endlessly rediscovered, her great beauty. The galvanizing simplicity of her skin, her smell. But to love a woman to distraction you must feel some lack; parts of her must elude you. She was too much his — like his own body. Even at moments like this, when she went scampering off to the other end of the room, she gave a curious impression of being his exact copy. His little ones were more lovable. They were as pretty as a pair of dreams, his two devils; they were not too much like him. Dadou hated anything to be too much like him. That was putrid.

'Do you want the blue jacket, darling?'

'No.'

'The light brown?'

'No! For formal occasions you wear white.'

'But white makes you look such a sweetie.'

'So what?'

'Darling! Personally I like a man who makes you really want it. Not one of these dolled-up posers. I want my man to make other women crazy for it.'

He looked at her and wanted her. But there was no time for anything now. He focused all his desire in one small kiss that he planted at the base of her throat. She quivered. She wanted him to prolong the embrace. Dadou, aware of the power of that body, decided not to risk granting a prolongation. He would miss the commissar's party — which would involve not complications exactly but an element of disgrace. You always needed someone more important than yourself. The country was a bit like that. Why contrive exceptions? Especially unnecessary exceptions.

'Ah, darling!'

'Yes?'

'Will you . . . be back late?'

'If the party's not too putrid. . .'

'You don't desire me the way you once did.'

'What do you mean, "once"?'

'I don't know. Oh, I don't know. But I want you to desire me in a really powerful way. All that time turned to night around me, the time when I was a firm-fleshed girl, a climate of flesh, evening burning in my body, my body burning. . .'

'What's for lunch?'

'Wh. . .'

She gave him a long look, bringing her whole body to bear in a final effort of will. But Dadou repeated his question.

'Beans,' she said.

'What have you put in with your beans?'

'Buffalo.'

He liked beans. But with buffalo. . . He was going off meat. With his new way of smelling, when he ate meat it said something to him about his own flesh. It smothered him, encircled him, gave him a feeling of wretchedness — a sort of insecurity complex. He was no mystic, but was this a discomfort with the whole physical side of existence? Perhaps not. At times, though, he felt like a stranger in his own body, and he was beginning to find that 'plaguey'. He liked the word 'plaguey', as he did the word 'putrid'; he found them shrouded in a curious magic; they split his whole being in two, and between the two parts, which were as strange to each other as to himself, there was a bright core of nothingness running right through him, a belt of nothingness that had to be stocked with something — something from inside himself, something he had never found. Try as he might: his left hand, his foot, his heart, tiredness, work, wine, dancing, women, the putrid, the plaguey — anything rather than the emptiness, because emptiness kills and confuses. Emptiness is the mother of despair. Dadou made great efforts not to despair. Even as life fell away he would still believe in it.

Lunch had been late. He had had to eat his beans hot in order not to miss the speech and the family's public coming-out. He would not have slipped his two zaïres into the commissar's mouth in the hope that he too would 'come out'. Dreadful custom! It is considered a disgrace if a guest does not slip the person coming out of mourning a little banknote by way of congratulating him on his fine clothes or his excellent dancing. This invasion of money into everyday life is something the Belgians left us as a mark of love. A mark of soul. As four o'clock approached, Dadou had left his dessert uneaten. He had not even stopped to scold Lola for having laid out his light brown suit instead of the formal white one.

He had been asked to sit at the head table, right beside the commissar, in the palm-branch hut erected for the occasion, right opposite what was to be the dance floor. The girl sat on his left. She smelled very good. Around the table Dadou recognized a good many quite high-ranking military and political figures. The municipal commissar was among the most important of those present — if you reckon that generals, too, are important public figures. The speech concluded, the members of the deceased's household 'came out' in line, dancing to the rhythm of the Almighty OK Jazz Band. The band occupied the upper floor of the commissar's large house, in which passers-by thought they caught the occasional whiff of petty cash diverted from the public coffers. In fact the commissar, even if he did not entirely look like it, was a solid, honest man. But in these young countries it was wise to assume straightaway that those in responsible positions were crooks. They had certainly done everything to acquire that reputation, and they went to great lengths to preserve it. Some even sank to confusing completely what was theirs and what was the nation's. They thought, rightly or wrongly, that personifying the country meant simply managing it as one managed one's left hand or one's right foot. They *were* the nation at certain points.

Dadou was irritated that the commissar was not dancing. He got up anyway and went and slipped his two zaïres into the mouth of the first woman who came to hand. The woman showed surprise. She did not know him. That kind of money could come only from those who knew you. She searched her pretty head, her pretty body, but found nothing. She would offer him a dance to clear the matter up. He had an attractive physique, after all. A noble air. And, as the saying went, he was the kind of man who made you want it like hell. She smiled at him. Awkwardly, Dadou returned the smile. He assumed the woman's husband (such a stunning woman had to be married) must be watching her every move. What a putrid world! Dadou smiled to himself. The young woman accepted this other smile, too.

The band had launched into a second and then a third number. The dance floor was teeming with a rhythmic crowd of happy 'bumpers'. The 'bump' was the latest Zaïran dance, having ousted the 'cavacha' and the 'jerky ekonda'. Why it had conquered all ages was because after the rumba it was becoming our least athletic dance. You bumped by rocking your hips from side to side. Your arms and legs were reduced to rebellious, disorderly, intransigent waves of flesh and bone while your head bobbed like a cork on the waters of the movement below. Contact between partners took place uniquely in combinations of gestures amounting to a whole sign language of question and answer: you suggested yourself to your partner, you suggested your warmth, your intensity, your total physical presence. The kid was bumping with a good-looking young man in dark glasses. For her, though, the dance was one of pure formality; it was clearly giving her no pleasure, in fact she was waiting for the end of the piece, while the young man was knocking himself out.

'My niece there — she's one to watch, Citizen Principal. She's got the poetic itch, writes some very good lines sometimes. No, she'll never teach. I only sent her to teacher-training college for her to learn something. You know what I mean? It's the way to the top, teaching.'

'Teaching rather less than the army.'

'She's no slut, either — she's got character. She says she's still . . . intact. The doctor's confirmed it. Of course, it's not going to be easy, finding a solid enough man for a woman of that calibre. It was she asked me to invite you. She was sure you'd come. Are you married, Citizen Principal?'

'Yes.'

'Children?'

'Two devils.'

The woman to whom he had given his two zaïres came to ask him for a dance. Dadou was going to refuse, but the commissar threw him a meaning look.

'This is Yealdara, my eldest daughter,' he said. 'She dances very well. She won't disappoint you.'

Dadou got up. The band played a rumba. It was a long rumba; it went on and on, with the couples dilating, lost in the tangle of sound. A long, long rumba. Long, full, and taut, the bodies dancing.

'Are you a friend of my father?' Yealdara asked.

'No.'

'Was it he invited you?'

'Yes.'

'What is your name?'

'Dadou. Citizen Dadou.'

'Dadou. Do you know me?'

'No.'

'And the two zaïres?'

'I was going to give them to the first comer.'

'Are you married?'

'Yes.'

'Are you happy?'

'I don't know.'

'Have you tried to find out?'

'No.'

'You're a coward, Citizen Dadou.'

'So what? Cowards breathe too.'

'My name is. . . Ah, my father told you. Still, I'd like you to hear it again: Yealdara. I'm reading for a doctorate in sociology. I ditched my fiancé because he didn't do enough for me. No personality. A slogger physically but otherwise just dim. I should have someone with more spunk. A fellow with blood in his veins and ideas about something other than, say, money.'

The band began a 'bump' rumba. Dadou did not want to dance this number but she made him. Yavelde was now dancing alongside them, partnered by her uncle. The West's contribution, that! In the old days, when fathers or uncles danced nieces were not even allowed to watch. Nowadays, to cap everything, nieces danced with their uncles. It is called 'civilization', apparently, and these people who have had only a very short course of it tend to get into rather a tangle.

Dadou had to admit that Yealdara danced very well indeed. She was generous in all her writhings, quivering in a way that was almost outrageous. The kid was incapable of hiding her jealousy: her movements were becoming agitated.

'What do you do, Citizen?'

'I'm principal of a college. A girls' teacher-training college.'

'You must be used to pretty faces, then.'

'Oh, faces. . .'

'They don't interest you?'

'You could say that.'

'It would make you a most unusual sort of principal.'

'I'm not a virtuous man. I abhor virtue. But laziness, too, makes me sick. And I loathe sexual ostentation. Nowadays all women advertise their sexuality. They live very dispersed lives, sexually.'

The band slipped the dancers a slow foxtrot. Dadou looked up at the night. The lamps had been placed too far apart, evoking a certain weariness, a strange despair. It was as if some of them would not see daylight. They swayed to the voluptuous rhythm agitating each and every body, including those of the idlers swarming all over the walls of the property and hanging in delighted bunches from the neighbouring trees. Yealdara's question sprang up again deep within him: 'Are you happy?' He did not know. Life is like that. One often guesses that one is happy or that one is not. But does one really know? One is never sure of anything. You have to make a positive effort. You are happy because your wife is (or women are) sleeping with you satisfactorily. Because money is plentiful and your friends are pleased with you, or because your car hardly ever breaks down. You are happy because the food you are eating and the wines you are knocking back are both excellent; because your health gives you no cause for concern; because the rhythm of the band is afloat inside you. You are as happy as a tadpole. But who knows whether you will be a frog or a toad? Dadou was a man who made demands of life. No doubt that was why he did not know whether he was unhappy or happy.

'You are hard on women, Citizen Principal.'

'To be hard you have to judge. I don't judge. I observe, I take note. And I react. A gut reaction — of the flesh rather than the intellect. Do you see what I mean? Women are something you knock back like wine and afterwards you have a hangover, you feel sick. I don't like feeling sick. The whole world, life itself — just so many ways of feeling sick. You think things out. When you do that you inevitably fiddle the sums — you forget the decimal points. And you arrive at a world in a state of catastrophe. I'm not a catastrophe; I'm a live human being — a normal human being, even, not a creature of formalities. I'm flesh and blood — strong flesh, too, not something you go looking for up there: something inside me. It lives in me, my flesh, it sleeps with me; we arouse each other. We know each other.'

'I'd like to sleep with you to see if you're a knockout. . . How shall I put it? You monologize so much. . .'

'A knockout? Yes, I knock myself out as well. But it's a fluke.'

'Let's dance this one too, shall we?'

'No, I'm tired.'

'The next one, then?'

'I'll not dance any more this evening.'

'You make me regret that.'

'So what?'

The commissar pointed out that they had made a splendid couple. But Dadou was not listening. He was keeping a listless eye on Yealdara, who was now dancing with a tall young man of about twenty-five. She 'bumped' well. The commissar was visibly proud of her. Everyone acknowledged that his daughter possessed disturbing features, forming a delightful harmony, and that she knew how to use them. Some eyes widened at the sight of this man (not bad-looking, at that) who had managed to keep her dancing for hours. She was a whore, maybe, like all women, but a whore of the higher moral spheres, a whore of life's wide-open spaces; and to get there, into life's wide-open spaces, called for talent and patience. Here was neither talent country nor patience country; this was easy street, this was a fine place, where you could be easily happy or easily unhappy. Decent enough folk, though.

The kid came up to him. She took his hand and asked him to dance. He felt like saying no, but once again the commissar intervened and in a moment their two bodies were fused together, choking beneath the beat, yielding here and there, giving occasionally like old thatched roofs. She took too firm a stand inside him, her flesh setting up eddies in his that tumbled his thoughts. He tapped the word 'kid'. It rang with a tragically weakened sound. He thought about his wife, then about his two devils: it was good here. It was good there. It was good everywhere, come to that. He still felt putrid. He even had the idea that he was nothing but a brief biography to be recited from beginning to end. The kid's body struck him as contagious. It showed him ways forward, gaps, apertures: a great craving of the spirit.

'Does she dance well, my cousin?'

'Yes.'

'She collects men, you know.'

'So what?'

She conveyed her whole body to him in crazy gestures, diabolical combinations, dizzying urges. How putrid that he was 'charm-proof', putrid on every level. Actually, Dadou thought, his fear of the kid was simply the other face of his 'putridity'. He wished he might be swept along by the rhythms of that implacable young body; life did not even give him the chance of letting go. He would have done so willingly, with a talent and possibly a passion for it. In order to quench the body that was taking fire in every corner of his soul and etching itself into him, Dadou drank an impossible number of whiskies, beers, glasses of wine. . . At four in the morning his own body slipped from his grasp: he collapsed in the middle of the crowded dance-floor. He felt hands all over him. Feet, too.

Voices saying it was stupid to drink when you didn't know how to. People groused, people mocked, people yelled abuse. The image of the girl had driven deep inside him.

'He's puked, the bloody idiot.'

'Mind your shoes.'

'Filthy swine. Filthy bloody swine. He's fucked up my best jacket. Let him have it!'

Dadou felt the blow strike his body. In the ribs. But he felt no pain. It would have taken a harder blow than that to rouse any part of him. Sleep was blotting him out. He wanted more than anything to wake up. Drink another whisky, another glass of wine, dance another dance. But sleep sucked him down into its dark abyss.

He woke up on a little couch in the commissar's luxurious drawing-room. A clock made twelve assaults on his ears. He still stank. Yealdara came and sat by the bed. She was wearing a dressing-gown. Dadou took her hand. She gave him the other one. Yavelde eyed them over her book.

'Why do you drink so much?'

'To piss on virtue.'

'Do you succeed?'

'I try. That's what matters.'

'What is this, Dadou?'

'A hole.'

'A hole in society?'

'No.'

'I'll bring you some coffee.'

'No.'

'Something else?'

'No.'

'What do you want, then?'

'I want to go home.'

'All the others have gone to pray for the memory of the

deceased. You must wait for my father.'

'No. I must go home.'

'Have a shower, at least.'

'No. I'll go home like this.'

'In those clothes?'

Yavelde tried to stop him leaving. Dadou, however, gently pushed her aside. He staggered as he walked away. A diadem of flies set off his silhouette. And if he fell, somewhere out there? God grant it was not under the wheels of one of those Japanese cars now clogging up the town.

'That's a handsome wreck,' Yealdara observed.

'He's a man,' said Yavelde. 'There are not many left like him.'

4

Dadou was having difficulty in sustaining his old work-rate. He had taken to arriving late — unheard-of for him. For three months now things had been slipping.

'Putrid's changed a lot,' the girls told one another.

'He's losing weight.'

'He got pissed at the commissar's coming-out-of-mourning. And I mean pissed. He even puked over people. They tossed him around like a cork. He stank.'

'Three months ago he didn't touch alcohol.'

'Nothing unusual for a beginner.'

'But why should he start belting his liver all of a sudden?'

'They say he and his wife have the knives out.' (Laughter.)

'Men are an item you don't want around the house. They're sweeter in the street.'

He was the talk of the neighbourhood, too. Dark talk. And matters went further. Often — too often — the talk in government departments is of football or drinking, occasionally of women. Departments with a lot of women talk about fashion and the latest superwax. At the Ministry of Edcuation they talked about the Dadou affair. Before, the man had been known there as a model of discipline and gravity. People used to say that Dadou was not altogether a child of our century. And the hundred-per-cents his college scored in examination results were put down to the character of the principal, notably to his intransigence. They gave him the nickname 'the old man'. The angel, however, had come a cropper, and this morning the director-general had asked to see him.

As he went in Dadou recalled that the teacher-training college was still the consecrated property of the Swedish Mission, even if the government did have full control.

'Citizen Dadou? We don't like to be critical. But when the whole town complains about a person, the time has come to tell that person that no one in this department is irreplaceable. You would do well to change the way you're running things. We set great store by the reputation of our teacher-training college for securing the future of all who graduate from it.'

'I've reached this point in my life, Citizen Director-General. Something tells me I have to drink.'

'At the risk of losing your job?'

'Why not?'

The director-general knew Dadou. He knew something pretty bad must have happened for him to talk like that. He felt a degree of affection for this man who was clearly coming apart fast. The fellow was a mess to look at, though.

'What is the matter with you, Citizen Dadou?'

'My life.'

'Too much stimulation?'

'It's starting to crowd me, flay me. . .'

'Listen, I've got it — I'm a man: I could help you.'

'Thank you, Citizen Director-General.'

'What is it, then?'

'My life.'

'Debts?'

'No.'

'Trouble at home?'

'No.'

'You look like someone who is contemplating suicide.'

'What's the use of committing suicide?'

'I don't know. I don't know. Anyway, if ever you need help, don't hesitate. We know you well. Known you since Independence. You've always been a sound citizen. When was it you took your first drink, exactly? Maybe two months ago, not more. And now you stink of the stuff. And your college is starting to go downhill. Absenteeism has set in, and you have indiscipline and immorality. It's a true word that when the stake leans, the plant leans too.'

At this point Dadou smiled — without in fact knowing quite why. And the director-general flew into one of his rages. He practically insulted him.

'You're leaning, Dadou — you've been leaning for four months. And when someone puts himself out to offer a helping hand you laugh in his face. You shit in his hand. Well, if you don't change, if you don't straighten up and do it quickly, I shall find myself with no alternative but to sack you. A girls' college principal has to be someone. He has to be a man. Now. We don't need any "has-beens" in your job. You may go.'

One phrase went on ringing in Dadou's ears: has-been. There was some truth in that. Some. Probably because at the age of thirty he had been made a Commander of the Order of the Leopard. It was a distinction he owed to his feet — to his left foot, to be precise. For thirteen years he had been the idol of the football stadium. His country owed a great many trophies to him. But then a nasty fracture had put paid to everything. It had happened during a Zaïre-Congo match. The whole stadium had wept. The Congolese as much as the Zaïrans. Dadou, too, had wept for his foot. He loved it. It was with that bit of his body that he expressed himself best and could persuade others and convince himself that he was good for something. It was with that part of his anatomy that he managed to deal a huge blow at inanimate matter, broadening the sound of his own breathing. And if up there in the higher echelons of the regime there were people who remembered him, it was on account of that portion of his anatomy. Dadou thought back to those times when thousands of pairs of lungs had hung on a movement of his foot, the stifled moment before the explosion of that awesome 'Whooo!' that greeted his goals. His leg gave an involuntary jerk. He would have played the World Cup if chance had permitted. He had played against Pele and won.

Has-been. He had been a minister. Minister of the Leather Sphere. Someone might have written his life-story. Why did he drink, in fact? The itch. The urge. The girl, too — her above all. He had to forget the kid.

'Drop me here,' he told the driver.

He went into the *Magistrate*, where the proprietress knew him already, and sat down in his place. His place. The one he had not found anywhere else in the world. Not even on the football field.

'Well, big fellow?'

'My usual.'

'I've got some new things in.'

'What?'

The woman leaned forward to speak in his ear. This was not a name for the cops to hear.

'Prosonty el cuensa.'

'What's that?'

'A spirit made from maize, tobacco, cassava, and wild herbs — gives you a lovely feeling. Otherwise known as "itch vapour".'

'What does it sell at?'

'Three zaïres a shot.'

'I'll try it.'

The woman brought him the drink with two pieces of lemon on a saucer.

'It's fantastic with lemon.'

Dadou tried it without lemon first. The woman was right. The drink definitely had something. He ordered two more. He preferred it without lemon.

His brain was beginning to dissolve presences, so Dadou stopped. He was not afraid to go on. His mind acquired enormous virility in drink. But for the sake of the job he got to his feet. The proprietress brought him one last sip, which he swallowed standing before he signed the cheque for the week's drinks.

Outside, the light had a dislocated quality. Dadou rubbed his eyes. He saw a man in front of him, a kind of giant holding a large knife from which blood was running in a bright red stream. Dadou rubbed his eyes. The man licked the knife and smiled. As he came closer, Dadou saw a small boy. The boy was playing Indians with his friends. He was holding a bunch of red feathers. Dadou rubbed his eyes.

The child smiled at him. 'You're going to fall over, mister.'

Soon Dadou was surrounded by small, feather-trimmed faces. He was helped up, but the world continued to pitch around him. Everything was liquid, undulating — streets, trees, houses, sky. Things became so dense that Dadou lost all headway. Outside the entrance to the college he sat down on the kerb, legs in the gutter. He slept, the ten o'clock sun burning his lips. Flies were feasting on the corpse of a cat just beside him. One or two of them took a chance and settled on the cracked lips of the sleeper. Beyond the wall, bells were ringing.

'Putrid's not here this morning.'

'It's odd. He's been making a real pig of himself lately.'

'Putrid's a saint. It seems girls — even pretty girls — mean nothing to him.'

'You've tried?'

'Who in this college hasn't? We all dream about him.'

'You're right. The commissar's niece melted quite a chunk of the monolith, though.'

'She's beautiful.'

'So am I.'

'She's really beautiful.'

'Yes, well, I could teach her a thing or two about technique. You know the minister? He's after it in earnest now. Comes round every evening. He's even mentioned marriage. I'm thinking it over. It'll mean giving the other one the push.'

'The other ones, you mean.'

'What, those studs? I'm talking about Simani. My parents know about him. But if I bring them a minister in place of a Treasury clerk, they'll take the minister. That doesn't stop me loving all the handsome fellows in the world. I have a weakness for good looks. You know me, dear.'

'Putrid's very good-looking, too.'

'Yes.'

'There was a time when I thought I was in love with him — hysterically.'

'So did we all, dear.'

'You don't feel much of an urge for a fellow who's going to puke in your mouth. In fact, that's a good way of fighting it. There's a real way of fighting the body — because it's stubborn, the body is. But do you think he's impotent, then, your Putrid?'

'He has a wife and two children.'

'Huh! You know how they do that, don't you? They have a cousin or a close friend come round and screw you to get children — between filthy tricks.'

'I danced with him at the Citizen Commissar's coming-out-of-mourning. I rubbed so effectively I got him quite aroused.

He was giving off a real charge. A nice bit of local heat. It felt good and solid through my dress. It was making me swell up, too. The top part of him stank of booze, of course. But I was almost jealous of the girls who danced all night with him. You know the commissar's daughter? The intellectual? She was making up to him all night. So was Yavelde.'

Midday struck. The doors were about to open. People had already stopped their cars and motorcycles and were preparing to pounce on girlfriends who in addition to their bewitching bodies possessed the not inconsiderable asset of a financially secure future.

Dadou stood up. He staggered to the entrance. Objects and people were less liquid around him. Everything was settling down except his legs — and his mind, still buzzing with the director-general's 'has-been'. Why should he be an 'all-time' man, anyway? He saw the kid's face spring up in his unsteady mind. She was crying. Dadou looked at her for a long time. He felt despicable. The lowest of the low. But that was fine. That is excellent, he thought. Let her fuck off, then. I refuse to fall in love. Never let a kid get her hands on your balls — she may chuck them anywhere, and you'll have a job collecting them up again. I've said it before and I'll say it again: man is noble only when he knows the price of choice.

5

Three months. The proprietress of the *Magistrate* was amazed.
There was the man's place. But the man had stopped coming.
He was still ahead on the slate. Twenty zaïres. Yavelde knew
the bar. This being vacation time, she no longer saw Dadou.
She took to waiting for him in the *Magistrate*. In vain. The
proprietress always told her to drop by again. And she did. She
would go on doing so as long as she lived. It was becoming
almost a way of life.

'Evening, Aminadou.'

'Citizen Dadou! You've been avoiding us.'

'Pressure of work, my dear. . . The usual. Do you remember
my last usual?'

'I do. Only the cops have been sniffing around, and we've
shifted our stocks as a precaution. Tomorrow we can take the
risk. Tonight you'll have a kazumurachi. That's a nice drink, a
kazumurachi.'

Just then Yavelde came in. There was a sublime quality in her face, a touch of wildness in her walk; she was madly attractive. Dadou swallowed his kazumurachi at a gulp and ordered another. Yavelde came over and sat down. Her mouth was soft. Her whole body seemed to be kneading a dull pain.

'A juice for her,' Dadou said.

The juice was brought. The record-player spun a Tabu Ley hit. Dadou was crazy about the piece. He hummed along with it. The atmosphere was less cheerful when the proprietress put on *Mokolo na kokufa*:

> There are days
> When I think
> I am lying there
> The way I'll lie
> The day
> I die. . .
> Yes to your tears
> Though I'll not even know
> Who weeps
> As I lie there dead. . .

'What are you doing here?'

'What are girls of my age usually doing in bars?'

'Why this bar?'

She was silent. A fierce, woman's silence. Body and woman. Or rather body on the verge of becoming stunning woman.

The bar filled up with a happy, joshing crowd. However, it included neither the giants of this world nor the fat crabs of the higher echelons of politics. Any more than you would have found the loonies of the younger generation there. This was a haunt of men who had found their moral and social feet. There were the special customers and their special tastes — those who paid in advance, it might even be by cheque, or who drank before paying at the end of the month. Some had one or two months' credit, the proprietress knowing they would pay: they would have paid but for this wretched death in the family, or that uncle who had arrived from the village, or the other illness and the medicine prescribed by the doctor at the Mama Yemo Hospital. Eventually a month would come when they sent everything else to blazes in order to settle their bill. They would tighten their belts, as the saying went. Or they would simply borrow elsewhere to pay here. People used to say that a man from these parts was a hundred times cleverer than his wages. They were right. He spent his life flogging his wages to death, yet there had never been a case of wages biting anyone. Or rather they did bite, but it was never fatal. They held back.

'What's the matter with you, running around after me like. . .?'

'Can't you see?'

He said nothing. That is to say, his mouth said nothing. He emptied his kazumurachi and ordered another. The proprietress was delighted with him, drinking three at that speed! She promised him one on the house. Dadou emptied his glass and asked for the free one right away.

'Citizen Dadou! I'm running around after you because I mean to rape you.'

She burst into tears. She flung bundles of sobs at him. Dadou noticed that she had a wide cut below her left temple. He felt a surge of pity.

'What's this?' he asked, touching her temple.

The wound was very fresh and ran from her ear to halfway down her throat. There, fortunately, it was a little less deep.

'What's this?' Dadou asked again.

'A razor blade.'

'You shave?'

'Yealdara tried to shave me.'

'How foolish!'

'We fight over you.'

'It's the sort of thing little girls do.'

'You see little girls everywhere. That's foolish, Citizen Dadou.'

She got up and left, taking small, tense steps — hoping he would call her back. Dadou called for a kazumurachi. The proprietress brought the drink with a professional smile. Dadou, beginning to feel drunk, fingered her buttocks. She sat on his knee. Yavelde turned away. It was too obvious. She walked straight ahead like a madwoman. Anger rumbled and boomed through her whole body. Anger and disgust.

'Go away! Go away!'

The words gave a shock to her throat like a strange ball of fire. They set her whole flesh raging.

'Go away! Go away!'

The words shook her and left her feeling feverish. She walked into the night. She walked all night. N'Dolo was the smartest of the bunch of boys who paid regular court to her. He lived not in Kalamu but in Matete. That was a long way, Matete. A very long way. But Yavelde had decided to go and sleep with him in order to mend at least part of her body, stop it melting away, stop her raging body escaping her control. She walked as if mad, arrived at nine in the morning, found the street, then the number. A young man of twenty informed her that N'Dolo had left for the Congo, where his uncle had died. And that, what with the disturbances affecting the river traffic between Kinshasa and Brazzaville, he would not be back in a hurry. Yavelde found the young man very attractive. She let him make love to her. On the way back she bore a double pain in her legs, a double weariness in her loins, a double nausea in her heart.

'They're looking for you everywhere,' the commissar scolded. 'I got the whole city out. And. . .'

'So am I,' said Yavelde, 'I'm looking for myself everywhere.'

She threw herself down on the divan and slept. She slept like a log. She dreamed of a number, a beautiful number: 6. She felt a twitch in her loins, a swirling sensation in her breasts. The golden age was lost.

6

The start of another academic year. A sickening bore. Dadou
was dreaming in his office in front of a stack of reports.

'We'll write the date, then,' came a Flemish voice from one of
the classrooms. 'Remember: a good hand is the best weapon in
a schoolteacher's arsenal. You there — look at the way you've
written the t and the d; you go at it too impulsively. Thursday,
24 September. . . And your 4 is like a miserable little tadpole. It
is not, by the way, the twenty-fourth today. Surely the least we
can ask of you in your examination year is that you should know
the date? By my grandfather's. . . What! You spell slate with a
y? What are you thinking of? And influence with two fs! Tell
me, did you pass your end-of-year exam or did you climb back
in through the window?'

'Fuck off!'

'What was that you said, my girl?'

'I said fuck off.'

'Are you aware of the meaning of that phrase?'

Anger stopped her mouth. Yavelde had a score to settle with all the men in the world. All of them. Whites and blacks. Belgians and Zaïrans. And Reverend Father Van der Weldyck had made the mistake of placing himself in the firing-line of her obsession. She had pulled the trigger: the loathing she felt for all men had gone off. She found him — as she found them all — vile, ugly, heartless. His only heart the shame of wearing flies.

'You're coming with me to see the principal.'

The Belgians disliked the word 'citizen'. It burned their tongues. Because of its political flavour. They stuck to the old form of address, despite the ban. The reverend father believed that the revolution here, like all revolutions, was just a fad and that, like all fads, it would pass. The world, to survive, must have everything pass through it. The only eternal truth was the disproportion between the human heart beating time and the dull throb of incorrigible, untamed matter.

'Come in,' said Dadou.

The reverend father related the occurrence to Dadou, who, having heard everything from his office, did not really need an account of it. He listened with only half an ear, looking at the pink scar that now disturbed the girl's features: her eyes, like her skin and lips, had lost some of their fierce intensity. It threw into relief little upsets in her facial movements, in the firmness of her bosom. That body, that small mystery, only recently so wild in every way and at every level, now breathed a bitter weariness. A weariness that sucked you down, as into a pit. Take an age falling in; spend your whole life on the brink. Dadou still had plenty of kazumurachi with lemon in his veins. The law, he thought. Nothing putrid about the law. The body, yes: all bodies are putrid. In fact, come to think of it, the body is the height of 'putridity'. The proof? The best proof is that it rises only in order to fall.

'Outside,' he told the girl.

She went, leaving the door open. The reverend father closed

it behind her. Dadou motioned him to a chair.

'Take a seat, father.'

He sat down. Dadou looked long and earnestly at him. They took each other's measure, as it were. Dadou began to smile, the reverend father to glower.

'Father, put this unfortunate moment behind you.'

'I beg your pardon, sir?'

'Forget the incident.'

'Do you suppose I came here to be insulted by Balubas?'

'That girl is going through a bad time in her life.'

'You're not giving me the reason, sir. I mean, you're not giving me the real reason.'

His big nose was alight now. He was sweating with rage.

'I know the real reason, sir, and I'm going to tell you what it is. We Belgians have never been afraid to speak plainly. You are defending the child because she's sleeping with you.'

Dadou was aware of all the kazumurachis he had drunk launching a combined assault on his nerves. He made to get up. His legs would not respond. His heart was almost bursting in his mouth. His whole head was awash with light, bright blood. Then, by a miracle, he cooled.

'Father,' he said in a flat voice, 'you talk so much about God, I believed you capable of understanding a man. Listen. I have committed a sin — a big one: I have not slept with that girl. And that is what is wrong with her. I'm suffering too — I'm going through hell. It's not for God that I'm denying myself, it's not for men, it's for nothing.'

The reverend father went out without saying a word. Finding the office stifling, Dadou summoned his driver. But Landu was not there. He'd have to give that Muyombe another bollocking. Dadou locked his office and started walking. Twice he just missed being run over. If he failed to punish Yavelde, the whole college would interpret his position as the reverend father had done. And the reverend father had not thought that up on his own. It was in the air. On Radio Street. Dadou cast around for

an appropriate punishment. Temporary suspension, stopping
her grant, making her apologize in public. He'd think of
something.

He walked on: not much further to the *Magistrate* now. He did
not even look where he was going. Someone threw him a 'Good
day, Citizen Principal' in passing. He nodded in reply,
unaware of who it was. He was thinking of this age and how it
pumped filth deep inside him, with girls swimming like
tadpoles in his blood. Their myriad different tastes and ways of
squirming. Of quivering, becoming distended. The multiplic-
ity. And the shapes of them. Perpetually new. Their wombs, the
root. It was all natural. Until the day he read this sentence and
decided to think about it: 'Among natures it is necessary to
choose the one that is useful. And among things that are natural
it is essential to opt for the one that is indispensable; that is the
way of wisdom.' He had persuaded himself that girls, though a
natural thing, were not the indispensable natural thing. He had
met Lola. With a horde of admirers. Some of them rather
assiduous. And, like every woman in the world, she lied. But
Dadou fell very much in love with her. He had begun by loving
her catfish smell. Then her moistness remained beneath his
fingers, her way of becoming aroused, her involvement in
particular moments of their frenzies, when she used to catch her
lower lip between her teeth to tease the pleasure out. They
reached it together, that sweet confusion of the flesh and the
void, that giddiness of the loins, that climbing of steep slopes in
the ultimate abandonment. Then Dadou had begun to find 'it'
a little tedious. He determined to fight, to crush this putridity,
but he came out of it with a tragic thread of flesh for drying
ideas on, strung taut, too taut. It was more stupid than the
putridity, particularly since beneath its sky he saw the sun of
the flesh but not that of ideas, the flesh being infinite and ideas
finite or on the way to becoming so.

'What are you doing here, Citizen Dadou?'
'I'm just off for a little drink.'

'And the job?'

'Indeed, the job. This body, though, is no longer quite the body for the job.'

'So the dark night of drink has got you too?'

'The day of drink. Not the night.'

'There is no day in drink. Presumably you have a particular problem?'

'I don't know what's happening to me exactly.'

'Drink, Citizen Dadou, is something that can come only from yourself. Even if this is the land of wine. Even if often — too often — the only place they all leave us here is muscadet and kalamashi: it is always a man's own fault if he drinks.'

'Will you join me, Citizen Zola? I'll pay.'

'No. I'm on my way back up. I went down too far.'

'There is no down in drink. Only dizzying heights. Pinnacles. The Himalyas.'

'After your problem you'll find the down in drink. I know that people here — the genuine ones — drink on account of a problem. Afterwards you'll be perched on a high wire of alcohol. Hundreds of metres up, and you'll feel dizzy looking at the city, the country, Africa. You'll say to yourself: they've done all that? How long have I been asleep in my kamurachi? She's serving you kazumu, I imagine? Or is it taka-ntambi? Unless you've gone for the white man's poisons, have you — whisky, port, gin, and the rest of that filthy stuff? Hah!'

The proprietress threw herself into Dadou's arms. This was not at all his time. Customers who came to you outside their time were to be made a fuss of. Her moist flesh jostled Dadou's. Deeply. More than just a woman, the proprietress of the *Magistrate* was a melting and most attractive immensity.

'Well, my lovely?'

'The usual.'

'The new one or the old one?'

'The new one.'

'You've nothing but trust left in your account.'

'That's worth more than money.'

'You pay like a white. I'll let you have it on tick.'

'You have a high opinion of whites.'

'Of everyone.'

'Whites wouldn't always pay if they were as poor as we are.'

'There are blacks wealthier than the whites and they still pay like blacks.'

'Bring me my usual. And push off with your prejudices.'

'With lemon or with sorrel?'

'Neither.'

'A real man drinks that kind of usual with lemon or sorrel. You're in perfect health and you have a horror of sleepless nights. At your age, with your great big body? You want to put years on your looks? No, I'll bring it to you with lemon. And if you still feel empty afterwards, if the other thing doesn't meet the case, I'll see to the rest for you. I've got what it takes there.'

7

'The date!' Reverend Father Van der Weldyk bellowed at the class. 'Today is Tuesday — Tuesday, 17 November. That's meant to be a 7? This class is a shambles. You — now I'm sure of it: some bigshot wormed you in here. You write like a spider, not even that well, so how did you get your place? By sleeping with some bigshot — am I right? And the bigshot slipped you your place. There's your Africa for you, your independence, your revolutions: it all starts between the legs. They ought to open a Ministry of Legs — that's where you belong. All of you. That's how you'll make it. Not here. Here you just fade. You turn "putrid". Silly bitches who spell orphan with an f. F for fools. You there! Are you going to shut up? Or shall I suggest you slink off to the principal's office? Oh, we've really got the dregs here. Sleep with the whole town and come into class worn out, stinking, and diseased. And I'm expected to teach you. What a laugh! They send me shit and I'm supposed to shape it

into something. You poor darlings — you've been uprooted.
You get yourselves slipped in here by uncles and cousins and
worse and told to be gifted, so bloody gifted — when all the time
your real gift is in your skirts. Your genius lies in your skirts and
in raising merry hell.'

Dadou, following the reverend father's lesson from his office,
had his head and eyes full of his usual. He had just arrived. The
old Belgian had doubtless seen him: much of the lesson was
clearly for his benefit. Dadou felt like creating a scandal. Going
into the class. Grabbing the priest. Giving him a bloody mouth
and making him eat his words, eat his whole wretched lesson. A
sentence drifted through his clouded mind: 'A disappointingly
large number of whites invite us to become racist.' Where had
he read that? Impatiently he reminded himself: an invitation,
for whatever reason, can always be refused. He fell back into
the reflections of Citizen Zola: the place, the only place left for
us is drink. But that was not why he drank. Dadou drank in
order to mire his heart (not his head) between that kid's legs.
His head was to scale but his heart was too huge, too greedy.
And to avoid becoming what he detested, that little wire for
drying ideas on, he drank — what other course was there? The
one his father had chosen: suicide? Someone knocked timidly at
the door.

'Come in.'

Miss Sayou came in, her face distorted by a violent panic.

'What is it?'

'The police were here.'

'What the hell were the police doing in my college?'

'They followed you to the bar. Someone told them you were
at the *Magistrate*.'

'Did they want to see me?'

'Yes, Citizen Principal. They said you were a murderer.'

'What do they mean, a murderer?'

She said nothing. They looked at each other, the secretary
trying to make out the features of a murderer, Dadou for his

part trying to satisfy himself that he was not drunk despite the morning's shots. She was reeling around in his mind, pretty much dissolved by the vapours of his usual. He attempted to repeat the word 'police' to see whether that had really been what he had heard.

'Either I'm dreaming, or your police have got it wrong.'

'All the same, you must make arrangements, Citizen Principal.'

'Arrangements? What sort of arrangements? And why?'

'I don't want you to be hurt, Citizen Director. You're a man of. . .'

'I haven't done anything.'

'The police are convinced you have. They would have beaten you in front of us.'

They are blind, like the law. And equally brutal. The only escape from the brutalities of the shabby law of the uniform is to be big — big as in bigshot. And there is also the communicable kind of bigness, the bigness through contact that comes from being a relative or friend of the original bigshot. Dadou remembered something else he had read: Africa, that great shit-heap where no one will take his place. What a putrid shit-heap the world was! Neither more nor less than a great big shit market. He imagined his wrists handcuffed, the blows, the laughter, the shouting. People going out of their way to insult him. What exactly was he being blamed for? His drinking habit, perhaps? But then why talk about murder? He got up and started walking. He walked for a long time. Maybe a policeman would call out.

'Putrid doesn't look too lively,' a girl's voice said.

'He's had a face like an owl lately.'

'You know it was him the whitethroats were after?'

He walked on. He thought about the proprietress of the *Magistrate*. Her hard smell, her belly in which it was easy to imagine the intestines, the excrement: you could imagine both their colour and their stench. Dadou composed his features.

The *Magistrate* was only a few more yards. Twenty. Maybe thirty. His flesh came awake. He would give those policemen a smell they wouldn't forget. He might even attempt to give them a good bollocking to justify the beating they'd be handing out to him.

As he sat down in his usual place a hand took hold of his. Dadou signalled to the proprietress with his free hand before looking up to meet the eyes of Yealdara. The proprietress spoke in his ear. She told him she had found something extremely rare: a 'usual' that, according to her, was good for a dry cough, tension, and impotence. Dadou ordered it. He was curious to 'sleep' with every drink in the world. Spirits, narcotics, whatever — to sleep with every drug, to kill life as one kills time.

'What are you doing here?'

Yealdara did not reply. She looked at him. Searching for something. Two measures were brought to them. Dadou drank them both, one after the other.

'What are you having?'

Yealdara did not reply. Dadou liked the new 'usual' very much. He informed the proprietress that it was a fine 'curiosity'. Out of respect for her customer she had called her new drink a 'curiosity'. Dadou downed his fifth measure. The proprietress, astonished at such speed, asked him if he was in a hurry.

'In your life you must never be in a hurry,' Dadou declared.

Smiling, the proprietress spoke in his ear: 'I had the police round, searching the place. I didn't think a citizen of your size would have that kind of bug up his jacket. What have you done?'

'Nothing,' Dadou said.

'Anyway, they laid about them.'

'What else are policemen good for?'

'You've done something to attract their attention.'

'Me? No, I don't think so. They must be making a mistake.'

'The police never make mistakes.'

Dadou drank his seventh 'curiosity'.

'Clever stuff, this,' he said. 'Instead of dissolving things around you, you drill through them, you firm them up. You go. Massively.'

He threw out a little laugh, which the proprietress caught and returned before leaving them alone.

'Yavelde's dead,' Yealdara told him.

'Dead,' said Dadou with a sigh. 'Good,' he added stupidly.

'How is that good?'

'I'm sorry, I'm drunk.'

'She left a letter.'

'For the doctors?'

'For the police. It . . . accuses you.'

'Who?'

'You.'

'Me? What of?'

'You told her to have an abortion. You supplied her with the means. But it went wrong.'

'That's absurd.'

'People are very angry. If they find you before the police. . .'

This town, this life, this world — they are full of innocents. Innocence, however, needs to be backed up by a bit of fisticuffs, a bit of footwork. He took her hand and began playing with the long, red nails. There was intoxication in those fingers, too.

'Do you think I'm guilty?'

'No. The police do. The family do. Everyone does, but not me. She and I used to watch each other, keep an eye on each other. I know she did it to get attention. But I can't prove it.'

'I can.'

'Let's leave. I'll help you.'

He hesitated. Yet he felt full of affection for Yealdara. She was concerned about him. Very concerned. Dadou did not love her. He went so far as to acknowledge the merits of her great body and the refinement of her soul. He looked into the hole that Yavelde made in him, a shit hole, a pit of excrement. He took a deep breath. Now he had the right to. His heart leapt in his great chest — explosion or release? A feeble voice issued from his dry lips: 'Yavelde, my love — why?' The 'curiosity' was making his head spin. Mechanically, he wiped away the tears that were running silently down his cheeks. A man of these parts, a Mukongo, doesn't cry. A Mukongo of the Kikwimba tribe, descendants of the monkey — he is a stranger to tears.

'I wasn't made for hell. But it looks, doesn't it, as if what I have before me now is hell.'

He was talking almost to himself. It was good to be talking to oneself — for the first time in years. It was even better to understand oneself. To size up what one said. To seize the precise scope and meaning of it. He hesitated again. His eyes appeared to shift in fury, deep in their sockets. No, it had not been him, Dadou, crying; it had been his condition, the 'curiosity'.

'We'll prove to the police that the letter is lying.'

'It will be difficult,' Yealdara said.

A hippopotamus of a man came over and spoke in Yealdara's ear. He whispered at length, gesticulating insistently, then walked away, chewing his lips.

'What did the citizen want?' Dadou asked.

'He's from the Special Official Etiquette Commission. He's looking for pretty girls for the presidents coming to the OAU conference. He's been after me for two days now. He wants to bring in a choice morsel so that he can pick up a fat bonus.'

'I wasn't made for hell,' Dadou repeated, more for his own benefit than for hers.

'No one was made for hell.'

'So why do people go there?'

Dadou ordered another 'curiosity'. His blood leapt in his veins, as if to say: 'You're just a coward, Dadou, a big coward.'

'I'm going to help you leave the country. I've prepared your getaway. There'll be a canoe ready,' Yealdara told him.

'Leave? With a felony charge against me? Never. They'll see I'm innocent in the end.'

'You talk as if you'd just arrived from the moon.'

Dadou bought himself another drink. Forty zaïres. The proprietress gave him an extra tot for being such a good customer. Dadou downed it in one. Things and people began to assume strange shapes: they started to fuse together. Dadou adored this liquid vision of the world.

'I've created hell,' he said. 'I've done it — I've created hell.'

'What for?'

'To keep going, I think. I could have been happy, but time . . . the gods . . . the law. . . I didn't manage it. A person can manage only one thing here: hell. And I'm happy to have done so. I'm totally content. Because here you either set up filth and excrement for yourself or you establish hell.'

Yealdara told herself it was the 'curiosity' talking, saying things without foundation. It was normal. The language of drink. Yealdara felt herself very much in love with this derelict. She recalled the day Yavelde and she had fought. Jealousy. She looked at Dadou. The body was sound, healthy, handsome, stunning, but the soul was rotten, she thought.

Rotten or. . . She was jealous of Yavelde. But she quickly convinced herself that in matters of love the dead were holes into which one could empty no matter what heart-felt — and gut-felt — emotion. She had faith in her great beauty. Men — all men — eventually succumbed to the snare of beauty. She would leave with him, cross to the other bank, the other side of the world. She would reclaim him from drink, deliver him from the law, wrest him from the dead and the living. They would build that world where the bed becomes compass and the sheets waves and storms, where smell is the wind and the body the whole universe. They would go dancing, drinking; they would leap streams, race through woods, pick their way amid crabs and boulders. You must put up a fight before you rot.

And if one day God takes pity on you he will raise you from the dead. Yealdara, however, did not believe in resurrection. Not, at any rate, as strongly as she believed in life, love, happiness, and the joy of giving. Her body intoxicated her, so great was her faith in it. She invested it with the rhythm of an intense aliveness.

'Have a little drink. It keeps things steady.'

'My thirst — my only thirst — is for love, for life. Spirits I can't stand — putrid, to use your word.'

'Love is another idiotic word.'

'No, you're wrong.'

'Why did she write those lies, then? Why did she kill herself? Why does she deprive me of my little hell? I was almost happy. I was making sense of myself. I was making sense of everything. Why has she wiped all that out? Why has she brought the world down around me, on top of me, inside and underneath me? Why has she left me this great darkness inside things and outside them? Why has she wiped out the world, leaving only the power of things, the "force of circumstances"? And this deluge burying me? And this *deconstruction*. And the fear of dying unfulfilled. Why has she made me curse her for a piece of trash, curse myself for a coward? Look at me — my body is exploding and slowly leaving me, bit by bit. My. . .'

'You've had too much to drink. Let's go.'

'Let me have one last mouthful.'

'The police and my father. . .'

'I've not done anything to the police. I've not done anything to your father. . .'

'You killed Yavelde. As far as the law is concerned, her letter is proof.'

'Oh, what rubbish! If I have to die, I'll die in one piece.'

Dadou swallowed his last glass of 'curiosity' and stood up. His legs were still obeying him. He walked in front of Yealdara. Out in the street the young woman hailed a taxi.

'Where are we going?' Dadou asked.

'To the river. You'll wait there with the fishermen while I get you some papers.'

'I'm not going to the river. Take me home.'

'They'll arrest you. And anyway, by now, if the police haven't been protecting them . . . your family. . .'

'I want to see what's left. Number seventy-two, Kabambala Street,' he told the taxi-driver.

The old Mazda groaned its way along the badly maintained streets — they were awaiting the next visit of the French president to beg the authorities for another bucket of asphalt, another lick of paint . . . Kalamu, South Yolo, Victoire. They took the left fork in the direction of the famous *Two-Four-Two*, the night club of the intelligentsia.

The taxi had been swallowed up on arrival by a furious mob baying for blood. Blows had rained down on it, smashing the windows and denting the bodywork. The police had dispersed the crowd only with difficulty.

The family was angry. The neighbours were angry. So were the jealous suitors. These people hated criminals, and whenever circumstances allowed they dealt with matters before the representatives of the law arrived. Yavelde had been a lovely enough girl not to be short of would-be avengers. The police had been stoned for protecting the three limp rags. The taxi and a police car were in flames. And the crowd was uttering cries of triumph.

'I got him a good one!'

'See this tuft of hair?'

'If I'd had a knife I'd have cut his tongue out. I had it in my hand.'

'I stuck a bit of wood in him. I'm certain something tore.'

'I had my razor — open.'

'If he doesn't die tonight he will tomorrow. I wrung his neck.

I felt this vibration in my fingers. But I squeezed. It went on vibrating. Still I squeezed. He's a tough one, though. They've all got tough hides — all the bastards. Did you see me squeezing?'

'What about me, then? Didn't you see me? I was trying to break his arm. But you're right, friend — the bastards are the tough ones. As the proverb says: "It's not the number of flies that makes the quantity of shit." '

The crowd went on talking till nightfall, the smell of the burnt-out cars heavy in people's nostrils. Laughter came from inside houses. Loud discussions. It grew late. On the cement floor of the police station, Dadou lay asleep. Beside the driver lay Yealdara. Before they found another place for her. Women's Rights Year: she was kept under close guard, close scrutiny.

In the morning Yealdara woke first. She felt pain, very recent pain, in her legs, between her legs. She tried to get up, lost her balance, and collapsed on the mattress laid out on the floor. She noticed a blood-streaked smear in the centre of the mattress. Rape. She spat. She felt she could spit out her whole body.

The policeman on night duty unlocked the cell. Dadou and the driver lay as they had been left the night before, one on top of the other, forming a cross of lacerated bodies. The policeman went in. Using his foot, he undid the cross of bodies. The driver moved one leg. They were breathing — that was what mattered. The policeman went back to read the charge that some fanatics had brought him in the small hours. Then he read the medical certificate before turning to the letter left by the deceased. The hand that had written it had trembled. The death agony, no doubt, or fear. Or it might have been anger or blindness.

I do not know what death is like. A river? A bridge? A wall? A door? I am afraid of it. But I am more afraid of life, this life in which I leave a loathsome monster: Nitu Dadou. A monster whom to my sorrow I loved with a sordid love. Everything is exploding inside me and all around me (my heart and my body are the size, to me, of the whole world). I'd have forgiven if I'd had it in my power. I tried: I could not. When your own smell is too much for you, when your mouth is too full of saliva and your shit overflows your guts, there is one course left to you: action. Denunciation, even if what you denounce is no more and no less than your own smell. As I write this letter, everything is fading into nothingness inside me and around me, everything is entering into absolute non-existence, leaving the field to my gesture, a gesture that draws deeply on my implacable woman's body, betrayed, deceived, annulled, unforgiving. And my bitter soul, my woman's soul, likewise unforgiving. The words I write here you will take no more seriously than footsteps in the street, no more seriously than a sip of Regla or Skol. They tell what was left of a body some described as radiant. They tell how I arrived in hell, but above all how I opted for hell. They show how I, a woman, tarnished hope, deliberately tarnished hope with a gesture that made me as crazy as my love, as ample as my body, as immense as my blood: I am taking my revenge. There is no other dimension to my despair: the body of love is about to crush the body of proud boasts. I was expecting a child by Citizen Dadou. One evening the brute came to me with some little pills. Because of his wife and children and also on account of the fact that he did not like polygamy, he asked me to swallow the pills in order to bring on an ab. . .

There the letter ended. The policeman smiled. Then he thought of his cursed relief, who had not turned up. Eight o'clock. Damn and blast the man! He consulted the rota: Dihoulou. He might have guessed. The squat fellow who walked like a chimpanzee and did not know the meaning of the word punctuality. The policeman bullied the log-book to take his mind off his impatience. He would go and take a bath. He loved to wash all over — after doing it. He bullied the drawers, the papers. He felt as if he was suffocating.

Nine o'clock. Dihoulou Toko wa Yala arrived for his shift. Yealdara burst into tears, sobbing violently. She had waited all this time. She had waited only to be raped, and by whom?

'Let's wait for the inspector,' the policeman said. 'Sit down over there. I'll do the report. You, the driver, and you, girl.'

There was an ants' nest right by the wall behind the policeman, at the entrance to the cell where Dadou now moved one of his legs. Mice were playing nearby.

Dihoulou Toko's assistant arrived at half past nine. He started bawling insults at the night-duty policeman on account of the duty mattress smelling of woman.

'See that, chief? This stupid Ibondi will never understand the difference between the station and the whorehouse.'

8

'What brings you to the law courts?'

Dadou recognized his old law professor from Lovanium University. Malvoisi had been his director of studies. He loved Dadou because of his ideas and because of his way of looking at and into people and things. He had also loved the title of his thesis: *The shadow of the law in the lives of criminals*. He had taken to asking as a joke: 'How's your shadow of criminals in the law progressing?'

'I'm on a murder charge. I'm the one who has been killed. That may be my fault. However. . .'

He outlined the situation for him in a few concise words. And Malvoisi easily established the innocence that was overwhelmed by appearances. A law has eyes only for appearances. And when appearances are against you, the law washes its hands of the outcome.

'Have you instructed counsel?'

'No.'

'Why not?'

'Money and time — time more than money. I asked a friend to get me someone. He went off with my cash instead. I've no one left outside now. My wife committed suicide after our two little devils were killed by the mob. Our house, everything we own — ransacked. They don't like murderers in this country. They only like virtue.'

'I'll defend you.'

'No, thanks. I want to get it over with. I've no one left outside — nobody and nothing.'

'You'll find them in the end. You must look everywhere, explore every avenue. Life is first and foremost a matter of curiosity, of questions about life, above and beneath life, beyond life, before, after. It's all there in your thesis. I thought you believed it. You used to invent the beyond. You made up the before and all the rest of it. So what about it, dear fellow? You don't want to leave something in the bottom of your life — you must empty it all. There'll be no one to drink what's left. Each and every life owes itself to drain its cup.'

Dadou felt a dryness in his throat. He looked around for the proprietress of the *Magistrate*, searching every corner of the courtroom, scrutinising every face. He swallowed his meagre, bitter saliva and could have traced it all the way down to his stomach and beyond. Malvoisi gave him a smile. Were they still in the same world?

'You've lost a lot of weight, Dadou.'

'You know, sir, sometimes I think I have no place either here or anywhere else.'

'They've broken you.'

'I don't know.'

'You have to know. And for that you have to stick it out, be determined, the way you were before.'

'Before was before. Today is today. Ah, if I could kill myself! But I see nothing in me to kill — it's all dead.'

'Dadou!'

'Don't mind me, sir. I'm talking about another world.'

'You just tell them I'm your counsel, that's all. I'll see to the rest.'

When the presiding judge summoned Dadou, Malvoisi intervened to state that he was not yet in possession of the documents relating to the case. He asked to be allowed adequate time, the case being a complicated one. He was given more time than he needed: nine months.

Back in his cell, the accused waited. His cell-mate tried to retrieve him from an abyss of gloom. The man's name was Falodiati, and his path to prison had been straightforward: he had laundered two million zaïres of government money. He was going to lose his case. Consequently he did not much care when they came to fetch him for the hearing. It would be a mere formality. Of course, when that formality becomes your whole life it starts to get you down. When you look around you, everywhere around you, when even the inside has crumbled and collapsed, there are moments when you feel afraid — afraid of yourself. Then Falodiati would grasp at Dadou as at a straw, for it is a hard thing to be shot for embezzling public funds.

'You know, friend, life outside — they have no idea of the value of it; they have no idea of the smell and the flavour of it. They crush it, they grind it to powder, or they pour it into women or into drink or food. In here, time is so dense you're afraid to drop anything at all into it. You're afraid of disturbing it.'

'Oh, I'm not afraid of anything. I'm waiting for my case to come up. I know it will come up one of these days. I've got a good lawyer. Malvoisi. Do you know Professor Malvoisi?'

'Everyone here knows him. The prison is full of university people at the moment.'

'Well, he's going to defend me. Then I'll try and start again. Start all over again. . .'

'Do you pray, ever?'

'I have been lately. But not to ask for mercy. I pray to ask God for some answers.'

'And does he give you any?'

'He will when he's ready. That's not my business.'

Falodiati had heard the news, but he was loath to obliterate the sole trace of life left at the bottom of this human object: hope. He had kindled it with his own hands, with his thinking and his reckoning, and he had told him so much about himself, his family, the local girls, the drink they got through at the embassy in Belgium, bands, horses, weekends at Matadi. But he declined to inform him that Professor Malvoisi had been repatriated because of his off-hand attitude towards the authorities. Almost three months had passed since the first hearing.

'The hearing is adjourned,' the presiding judge had said.

Yealdara had been called. Same story: hearing deferred until 26 January. On 26 January no one came to fetch Dadou. Time expired in his heart, in his head, in his legs. Real time, which he might have spent loving, drinking, living, dying. Yet even dying required solid, experienced people, Falodiati told Dadou. And Dadou said he was right.

'I had a nasty dream last night,' Falodiati said. 'A giant eucalyptus was growing in my throat, splitting it. Maybe it is time for me to repay my debt to the trees.'

A policeman came to fetch Dadou and told him the governor had asked to see him. Dadou threw his cell-mate a quick smile. He felt great affection for Falodiati. And if one day they managed to get out they would open a good bottle of wine together, maybe go and live in the country.

'Do you think it's your dream already?'

'I've got a shocking head,' Falodiati said.

Dadou wanted to say something else. But the guard pushed him on his way.

9

'Sit down, Citizen Dadou.'

The big body that had imbibed four years of prison bent in two as a skinny hand reached out idly for the arm of the chair. The chair made a scraping sound on the floor-tiles. Dadou stretched out his legs. A beard covered his chin. He reacted to the softness of the chair as to a woman's body.

His cock stirred. He crossed his legs to keep it quiet. The shame of it, in front of a man! The governor did not look up. He was tracing large black grasshoppers in a dilapidated ledger. Dadou calculated that the grasshoppers the governor was using for letters might perhaps beget good news. Five or six of them went to make up a name. The name of someone back there behind bars. Someone who was spending his life rotting away. Out here the writer was taking his time — for his it was. He went over each grasshopper several times. Then he drew some ants. Then some tadpoles. At five o'clock the man would go home. He earned his living on other people's time. He remembered the prisoner and glanced up at him. Pained by the sight of a man in such disarray, the governor went back to his locust-writing. He had privately decided to make conversation with the prisoner but could not think how to begin. Time went by.

'Did you step in something very nasty, then, out there?'

'Yes,' Dadou said simply.

'And your position out there is done for?'

'It may be,' Dadou said.

'You mean you'd like to go back?'

'Yes.'

'Why? Don't you like it here?'

'Out there or in here, it's still bad for me. But I prefer it out there because of the air and the sun. In here it's like rotting alive. You rot your nerves, your blood, your mouth corrodes. . . And your body, your own body grows like a weed. It has to be yanked out. All the time. Afterwards it itches.'

'Do you have someone out there?'

'No.'

'Some thing?'

'No. But I'll manage.'

'By drinking, for instance?'

'Drink is a thing, too.'

The governor, disturbed by the voice, looked up at the man. He felt a rush of pity. More for the voice — such a living thing! — than for the man.

'I like your name, citizen. It's genuine.'

'So everyone says.'

Once again the governor went back to placing his grasshopper-letters on the page of the ledger. Dadou was silent, listening to the unpleasant smells being secreted by his body. Male odours, bitter and repulsive. The scents of the office heightened rather than obscured them.

From somewhere inside him everything kept repeating: 'You

stink.' The two words stopped up his being with an unspeakable shame. How had he become this male object that was brought out and put back and was now growing hard? That would one day fall. But when and where? In what time? Under what skies? As God's or as the devil's?

'Did you really kill the girl?'

Dadou did not answer. He was thinking. The new captain of the Alleluia Thunderers. He had bawled her out after a defeat, and the girl had blown her top: 'You take us all for kids here. Well, I'm a woman.'

At the *Sportsman's Tipple* she had opened the dancing with him. Provocatively. Her every movement a snare: that too was life. The wench had nearly pulled off all her tricks including the button one, which was very elaborate. And it was at such hard moments that his wife stank of Belgians. . .

'You killed her, didn't you?'

'No.'

'Do you consider it was an accident?'

'No,' Dadou said.

'What was it?'

'A childish game.'

Once again the governor hid his eyes. He could not bear the sight of Dadou's face. The letters pitched about on the page as if they had become liquid. Here everyone is guilty, the governor thought. Directly or at a distance. But guilty. He went to a cupboard and brought back two bottles of best maize liquor. Dadou's throat stirred at the smell of it. He stepped out of his four years of cement. The governor poured him a shot. Dadou downed it in one. He did not wait for the governor before pouring himself a second, then a third shot.

'Who wrote the open letter to the governor?'

'The others. You know the prison is full of university people. And university people are full of ideas. They'll seize at the slightest opportunity for an intellectual brawl. It was my cell-mate who told them, and they blew their tops.'

'If they want to do you a service they'll shut up. As I was saying, your position outside is dead. It's closed. In here, as long as I'm here — no problem. They bring me money to let you out and allow them to bump you off. Two million, they're offering. I tell them: "In the name of the revolution, I cannot do it." Well, not entirely in the name of the revolution. I do things in my own name. I cannot sell a man. I was brought up to respect human life.'

He swallowed a shot, motioning Dadou to fill his glass.

'Do you smoke?'

'No.'

'The report says you used to drink like a fish. Why did you drink?'

'No reason.'

'No, Citizen Dadou. This isn't a country where people drink for no reason. Were you trying to drown your misdeeds?'

'I didn't kill her. It took me a while to convince myself.'

'That sounds odd.'

'The girl was in love with me — and I with her, come to that. I don't know why I wanted to try to be stronger than my heart, stronger than life. I can't say that life got the better of me, that life won, but I was shaken. It's a miracle I didn't shatter. I was almost proud of my old carcass. It held out.'

'She was a lovely girl. I saw the photos. One of those restless, sensual bodies. . .'

'Shut up,' Dadou said.

'That's a cruel thing, to murder a young girl.'

They sized each other up, then Dadou got to his feet. With an evident desire to fly at the other man's throat.

'Sit down,' the governor said.

'No,' said Dadou.

'I've something to say to you.'

'Say it.'

'You lied when you said you had no one outside.'

There were people. But they were people Dadou no longer

regarded as his. His people were dead: his father, his mother, his wife, his children, Yavelde. . .

'Aside from the ones who want to slit your throat you have other people out there who genuinely wish you well. A woman, for instance. A sort of nanny type. Between twenty-five and thirty. Acts like an old maid. Are you with me?'

'No,' said Dadou.

'A Jewish-sounding name.'

'Yealdara.'

'Right. She comes every day.'

'She's a friend.'

'I thought she'd been sent by the others. I was going to help myself to her. Grab the chance. All I got was a hard stare. She said she'd be back this evening. What shall I tell her?'

'Send her away.'

'She'll come back.'

Yealdara. Let her come, then. She could tell him what had been happening.

'I'm too dead for her,' Dadou said.

'No,' said the governor. 'This is heart, not skirt. Not tail, if you like. Tail you've got to go for in the conviction that behind it there's guts and shit. But heart is different. Heart is something beautiful. I like you, Dadou, because you came to prison down my road. No — people like us don't have a road. How it is with us, you move forward and matter germinates behind you. It closes up. It recovers its virginity. And you turn to find the death of the road. The world has closed off all passage — dense, untamed, terrible. And in front of you, all around you: untamed "revirgination".'

Dadou sank back into the armchair. The governor gave him a quick smile of friendship. He poured him the last shot from the second bottle, then went to the cupboard and came back with two more full bottles. The proprietress of the *Magistrate* crossed the prisoner's memory. Her image having melted the bars and kindled the reflex in Dadou's legs, the world was liquid once again and Dadou floating in it, infinitely fragile. Liquids have the advantage of assuming the shape of their recipient. Dadou felt he was about to assume, from one minute to the next, the shape of the world, of the country, of that society and its stupidities.

'Do you follow me? This place is almost home to me. I came here as a political internee — that's worse. That's filthy. Emptier. Like a puking in the brain. Day in, day out you become the prey of your own skin! I had the cell you're in now. I know how it bites. Four years I spent in it. When the new government came in they lent me a bit of outside. And that bit of outside I made the most of after my fashion. In our kind of society, you know, you've got to lay about you to find a bit of decent oxygen. Something that will let you move, get out from under people's arses. Eleven years I've been here. I watch. I see them all pass — the guilty and the innocent — geniuses, swindlers, ordinary men. Obviously, in a world where only the guilty belong, what do you expect them to do with the innocent?'

Dadou said nothing. He was studying the governor's hatchet face. What a man! His mingled smell of drink and cigarettes, his panther-like eyes, his ears, his reedy, friendly voice. Dadou found him wholly sympathetic. His flared nose, his greying hair, his cruel teeth. . .

'Do you follow me, Citizen Dadou?'

Dadou's mind was elsewhere. He was dreaming of the silvery shots he had been served at the *Magistrate*. He was dreaming of his team, the Alleluia Thunderers. They could be at the top of the local league. Those girls had been head-over-heels in love with him. Now no one, alas, thought of him any more. Yealdara. All right, but she had nothing to do with his beloved youngsters in whom he had invested so much protection, respect, and friendship. And who had perhaps all forgotten him. Why was the governor talking to him about life when he would rather have been dead? Life, for him now, was something almost external to himself. He was breathing. But so what? If they out there allowed him, he would return to the world. He would start again. The Alleluia Thunderers would be there. Girls who had some brains. More brains than bum. But first, if he was allowed out, he would go and have a special drink at the *Magistrate*. A big one — what we call a pope's tope. If the *Magistrate* had closed he would go elsewhere. He would enjoy again those marvellous moments that float and teeter and butt inside you. Those liquid moments in which everything is liquid. Liquidness in thought and word and movement, allowing both inside and outside to dilate. If he got out he would go and lay flowers on the graves of his two devils. On his wife's grave, too. If they had no graves he would throw the flowers on any old graves. They would have been buried by prisoners, using government sheets and deal coffins. The usual botched job, no doubt. He remembered an occasion when they had been fetched to bury the university rioters. The fellows had pinched the sheets and even taken the clothes off the corpses because June was a cold month in prison. Such 'recoveries' were routine. Everything was stripped from the corpse that could be of use to the living.

If he did get out, get home, fingers would follow him in the street: 'That man over there in the black *abacost* . . . with the red hair — he used to be principal of a teacher-training college.' And if it had been prisoners who buried his family — the shame of it! — he would not even know where. Prisoners never wash the dead. They leave them the way they met their end. Of the three sheets provided by the state, they take two — if they do not remove all three. It is cold where the dead go. Who has not heard of dead men coming back in dreams to beg something of a relative? But it is colder in prison. And since the dead man cannot defend himself he is stripped. He meets his fathers in the buff. They throw him out, and his ghost returns to haunt the neighbourhood. Those strange shapes you see drifting through the night in the early hours!

Dadou mused as the governor delivered a speech sustained by shots of maize liquor. He spoke as if to himself.

'Do you follow me, Citizen Dadou? I was saying the young woman should be here soon. Her time. . . It being eight forty-seven. . . Believe me, Citizen Dadou, you're safe in here. As long as I'm here, no one is going to touch so much as a hair of your head. Not even the President of the Republic.'

It was the drink talking. No one can rob the Good Lord of his love of creating. Whatever he feels like creating. And the governor was aware of that. Here the view of power is that the President will always be the father of all other citizens. Even when they do not become his things, they are still his children.

They waited until eleven o'clock that night.

The governor was half asleep by then. He invited Dadou to return to his cell: 'No, Yealdara won't come now.' The walk revived the smell of the *Magistrate* in the prisoner's loins. The scents of the fat proprietress came hammering at his nostrils. Made his legs itch. His throat felt dry. She sliced the world in two. In three. In several pieces. Then the cell sprang up in his heart and in his head. It occurred to Dadou that he would in the end get out of there, one day, maybe one evening. He would go and find out whether everything was dead for him out there, whether there was not something that could be resuscitated. The sounds, the shouts. The throbbing noises. And above all the Tabu Ley records that the governor's children put on every evening, every morning. He knew the words by heart. They were much too alive. Part of his life. As if at any moment a woman's voice was about to say to him, 'Citizen Dadou, will you dance with me?' The 'yes' hung in his throat. Ripening. Waiting. Like a foetus. But it was out there and only out there that that 'yes' would and could be born.

What path had he travelled in the depths of himself in four years? Occasionally his cock stirred too much. He whipped it or else squashed it between his body and the concrete until it shut up and left him in peace. Other parts of his body became aroused. Dadou spent much of his time putting out local fires. Then he begged sleep to come down and enter his eyes. But his brain was spinning at such a speed that he spent five or six sleepless nights before sleeping through one. 'When you can't stand any more, when you really can't stand any more, you'll kill yourself, like your father. And if death is as empty as life. . .'

Time traipsed on. In his head. In his belly. In his throat. Like a drove of days and nights. For supper they were often given rice. At lunchtime it was salted fish. Re-entering his cell that evening, Dadou found the usual aluminium dish filled with white rice. He ate the rice and fell asleep very quickly, thanks to the governor's shots of maize liquor. Anyone passing that way would have seen a ragged body, the head buried in beard and hair, shifting its position occasionally to drive away the nagging mice. The governor had given Dadou an old mat, and on this he slept soundly. He had also given him a cell to himself. And evil tongues had seized the opportunity to besmirch the governor for this excess of kindness.

Time dotes on the wretched. Dadou, however, had systematically searched all the time dying around him and not found a second that was his. Time had betrayed him and continued to betray him. Time had always lied to him shamelessly.

10

'As long as you're breathing, you're alive.'

Yealdara had taught him to say that. Thanks to the goodwill of the governor, she now saw Dadou every weekend.

She was deeply in love with him. Dadou, however, no longer had the kind of heart that loves. He had the other kind: the one that forgets. He was in the process of forgetting life, death, the world, nothingness. A situation approaching bliss if you can philosophize. But there was nothing of the philosopher about Dadou. He wanted to breathe and was short of air. He had tried to fill the gap with drink, but drink, too, had betrayed him. He had been told (and for him, now, that meant Yealdara had told him): 'Man comes into this world to love and pass on: to love everything — in passing.' Where was the time for loving, though? Dadou did have time for passing — laboriously.)

A man is in prison because others, outside, are drinking and bedding women, because out there dishes are steaming and songs being sung. A man is in prison for the simple reason that out there people are talking about football. And so they must. Otherwise the world would grind to a halt. In order that they may talk in peace, other people must lie on mats in prison, crushed. Yet there is nothing crushing them. No crushers.

Dadou got to his feet. Yealdara was still asleep on the mat. He woke her. They must avoid getting the governor into trouble. She always left at four in the morning, taking with her the smell of their two bodies together with that of the cell and that of the mat. Dadou knew, however, that she would go and wash. Out there, there was water. Lots of water. He kept the smells — one on top of another. And when the governor slipped him three shots of leaf spirit he used one of them as scent. Dadou still had hope. Yealdara had told him again, as had the governor, that his position outside was dead.

Yealdara's father was determinedly climbing the ladder of power. From being a municipal commissar he had become a district governor, then Minister of Information, and he was now an adviser to the President of the Republic. If he would only forget! But no: he remembered. And if he had decided otherwise Dadou would have been spared the little business of breathing. But he had wished him to stay alive — on a diet of concrete.

Hearing that the governor was treating his prisoner kindly, he had called in person to say, 'That piece of filth is my private affair. I want you to make things difficult for him.' Face to face with a minister the answer is always 'yes'. But behind the man's back the governor had done what everyone does and said 'no'. People like to disobey minor bigshots. They like to contradict them, think differently from them. For the governor, however, there was more involved than that simple urge. He was genuinely fond of Dadou and could never have brought himself to 'make things difficult' for him.

Yealdara had tried to reason with her father, but the old man had taken a very tough line. After that it was not long before the break occurred between father and daughter, he treating her like a common whore and she declaring that her father was the lowest kind of human excrement. Whereupon they turned their backs on each other; she went into the kitchen and wept. Her mother had died two years earlier. The then district governor had remarried: a sort of virgin of Yealdara's age. That had been the beginning of the father-daughter crisis. Yealdara had dropped her sociology studies. She wanted at all costs to get Dadou out of prison. To get him out of her father's clutches, free from the teeth of the town and its society. To give him back his taste for breathing.

Here — oh, yes — here she knew very well: to be alive was already to display genius. One must yell, as she had done with her father, howl in protest, whip up one's body, abuse it, or allow oneself to be trampled underfoot, reduced to a pulp. Dadou had fallen. The whole town was treading on him. Time, too. Life was walking all over him. The sun. The earth. Human bodies. Everything.

Dadou listened to the silence of time within his flesh. He staggered to the window. This — another present from the governor — was tiny and looked out on a field of barbed-wire entanglements and struggling vegetation. The sun was coming up on this mixture of metal and greenery, a mournful sun, rising beside a man who was there every morning, as he was this morning, signalling to him. But the signal was dissipated by the barbed-wire entanglements. The prisoner experienced a surge of anger. Why, for what rotten reasons do we come into the world? He felt like breaking something. But there was nothing breakable there. His leg, possibly. He really wanted to do it. But what was the use? He would have smashed his belly and his guts if that had offered a way forward. He so badly needed a way forward. A fleshway! A bloodway! Never mind where it led. Dadou wanted to move. Advance? Retreat? Climb? Crawl sideways? Move, anyway. He had been nailed down like a flap of flesh. Like a scrap of humanity. He wanted to hit on the way. He had moved inside Yealdara. But afterwards, their movements completed, there was the same cul-de-sac full of smells and warmth and itchy yearnings. He wanted to love. As with Yavelde. But the heart of love had gone. Leaving the other one: the heart of itchy yearnings. Dadou stirred up words but failed to make them issue from his throat. He swallowed them back down. A few shafts of sunlight forced their way in at the window. Dadou absorbed them as if they had been shots of leaf spirit. Large ones. He had made every effort to turn the window into an 'out there'. With less than one hundred per cent success, though. So much emptiness! So much nothingness! The fact that the governor now smuggled Yealdara into the cell added little to that hole of light pitting the prisoner's blind flesh. Time, to Dadou, was a slap in the face. Time hurt. It had become like a razor. . . His time hurt by that of others.

'I lost the taste for life in the taste for my destiny,' the governor had said.

It meant nothing, but Dadou enjoyed repeating the sentence to himself.

The governor came to the door of the cell. 'There has been a serious development,' he sighed.

Dadou said nothing. He looked at the governor admiringly. The man had something special behind all that flesh invading every corner of his body: he was there, as we say in these parts.

'A serious development,' the governor repeated. 'They're moving me. I'm sure it's to enable them to slit your throat.'

'Then let them slit it, and let's get it over with,' said Dadou.

The governor smiled at him: friendship. Ah, but how much should one take of it? Sometimes one was friends with a dog, a plot of land, a story, a moonlit night. . . One was friends with a failure or simply with a point of view.

'Only cowards think death is an answer,' the governor said.

'This world is meant for cowards. There's no room in it for anyone else.'

'Is that a reason for us all to become cowards?'

'I don't know,' said Dadou.

'I've nothing particular to do in life except to save people, when I get the chance, from being trampled underfoot. And there are my bottles of beer and my shots of leaf spirit. There's the Matongué district and the whores of Kalamu. There's Matongué Street and the Boulvelard of the Thirtieth of June. Beyond that . . . total blackness.'

At this point the warder arrived with a large bunch of keys. The governor made a sign to him. The man opened up and went away.

'I hand over on the fifteenth. That leaves me two weeks. A useful period. They'd have had you if they had given me less than three days.'

The governor took a five-shot bottle from his pocket and handed it to Dadou. Dadou, savouring the spirit, bit his lips.

'Prodigious!'

The governor smiled without reserve for the first time that morning. His eyes blazed like torches. He hugged Dadou with keen emotion.

'We shall fight,' he said.

'Prodigious,' was all the prisoner said again as the governor's hands busied themselves behind his back.

They will slit his throat, they'll do it, but he will have had several shots of spirit — which now seemed like several shots of world. Is that not what one comes into this life for? To drink one's shares of the world. Whatever they may be. Without confusing them with other people's.

'You're going out: out there Yealdara and you will see to the rest. I've already spoken to her about it. She agrees. With her so much in love, things ought to work out — if, that is, you make a big effort yourself. And if you want to feel safe, don't hesitate to cross the river. The other bank strikes me as a pretty feasible country. But you'll have to hurry.'

Dadou looked at the number on his door: 318 AF. His face cracked in a bitter smile.

'You wouldn't have another shot, would you?'

'No. I'm having something brought in this evening. But this evening. . .'

'Do you really think you're saving me?'

'No. At least they won't kill you with your hands tied.'

'I long for life. It's pathetic: a human has-been with an ardent desire for life. I loved the girl. And my wife. That seems inconsistent. But here inside me, under the skin, there's a connection — it all hangs together. All my dead. Ah, this hour moves in me like a force. And ahead of me time is silted up. Do you know what? I am so far inside myself that no one will ever again hear what I'm saying. I've foundered. I've conquered my passage here. It was splendid. It was courageous. It was great. But who am I talking to? Not to you. You cannot hear me. I am saying things that are eight hundred thousand years beneath your feet. The hole. My hole. It is so deep, and no one can jump into it except corpses, because even the mad are afraid to. For me, "out there" is like a hole. I congratulate myself on having the courage to jump.'

'Jump,' the governor echoed involuntarily.

'Jump. It's the action of the mad. But I believe it is also the action of poets, scholars, artists . . . it is even the action of God. I am performing that action. I am jumping. The tragedy is that I shall not fall. I am leaving. To each his road. On mine there will be Yealdara and the others. Oh, I wish I were mad, mad, mad!'

The governor locked the cell again. The keys clinked in his pockets. Distracted, Dadou's ears followed the sound.

He lay down on the mat. Maybe they would come. He hid his throat from view by sleeping on his stomach. He was aware of a powerful itch, as if it was already being slit. He pictured the blood, soaking through the mat onto the floor and congealing pinkly. How did a man leave life through a throat wound? The shots. All of them. Dadou had an infernal thirst. He would have drunk his urine if he could have been sure it contained so much as a trace of alcohol. His skull boomed hollowly. And he loved it. Ah, if only he could have gone mad.

'You're a plucky fellow,' he told himself. 'Plucky, heroic. Anyone else would perhaps not have toted this body so far. Anyone else would have broken down right at the start. But you have come through life and death. You are God. You have loved. You have suffered. You have been. You are passing through this dead body ten thousand years before yourself. And if they bring you down it will not be entirely you they bring down but your way. What does it matter if the way dies? The wake. The trail. They'll kill the trail, but what about you? They'll kill the shots; if the shots are dead already. . .'

Dadou spent the day as he spent every day, sleeping and thinking. In the evening the governor came back with five shots, which they downed very quickly. Then he handed him a pile of papers. Dadou opened the national registration card, then the party card, then the others. They were all there. The governor knew how to get things done. His new name — Sadi-Motara — made Dadou smile. Gently he touched his face with its advancing growth of hair. Fortunately no photograph was required on citizenship documents in this country. Only the name.

'We'll try it tomorrow night. The troubles with Angola have meant that the frontiers are being watched very closely. But with these papers you needn't worry about a thing. Your taxes and contributions are all paid up. Sadi-Motara was the name of an uncle of mine. He was very famous. I hope he'll bring you luck.'

He held out a razor and a pair of scissors, indicating Dadou's beard and long hair.

'Never,' Dadou said. 'They're my insignia. And anyway, I have an idea: if things turn ugly, I can always pass for insane. They don't arrest the insane in this country.'

'I should have thought of that,' the governor said.

'The shots you brought have only whetted my thirst,' Dadou told him.

The prisoner lay down on his mat. His throat itched and trembled slightly at the point where, if they came. . . The governor gave him an admiring look. It was the same powerful body, the same barrel chest, the same white teeth, the same eyes, the same scarred flanks, the same athlete sculptured in bronze like a Greek god. Dadou's hairy belly rose and fell with the rhythm of his breathing. He held the papers in his left hand, which lay a little beyond the mat. The hand that brings good luck.

'It's a tragedy,' Dadou said.

'It's a tragedy,' echoed the governor. 'But it's good that you are leaving. Outside you will make every effort, as you told me the other day — to breathe, to catch up on your oxygen. This is the land of struggle. You must dare to win. You must dare to go on. Or die.'

'I'm getting old,' Dadou said. 'My heart, my blood, my sinews. . . How can I make every effort at my age? I must find something to make me young again. But what?'

'Yealdara,' said the governor.

'With Yealdara I can't. . . If I could be madly in love with her! She's beautiful. She has great depth. But it's me — I have lost the hunger of the heart. The world is becoming a nauseating void. Everything is becoming nausea and emptiness. I've only one thing left to do here, and that is to submit to being nauseated. It's a wretched job. Here — take your razor away. It will give me ideas.'

'Dadou, you are a coward.'

'I wasted too much time being a stoic. You should have seen

me before. With the kid, for instance. With my wife, too. And throughout my childhood. It was all heroic stuff. Now I want a bit of rest. A day of rest in a lifetime of fire. Yes, you're right. Daring to win when I've no one in front of me. I'm an old fool, an old has-been. You keep me here — do you know that the real prisoners are out there, outside? Isn't that the most putrid thing? I'm no novice human being. Not me.'

They were 'outside' words. Dadou was aware of this. He had been using outside words for some time. But the outside — out there — no longer existed for him. He had been through that country: it was a country hostile to his solid build. Everything had shifted: time, hope, his luck. Everything had shifted by chance rather than through anyone's fault. Chance, however, was God. Dadou had good reason to believe that he was being pissed on by the gods of heaven, earth, and hell.

'Till tomorrow night, Citizen Dadou,' the governor said.

Dadou did not answer. He was thinking about Yealdara. A girl who really deserved to have a life begun afresh for her sake. But he had gone too far, much too far, farther than life. He could not come back now. There was only one thing he could do: stay in this other people's time that buzzed around him like a cloud of bees. Survive there as long as possible. He had the physique to survive. He lacked the heart. He'd get by, he thought. He'd make every effort. . . But how the hell had he become so insensible to beauty? Yealdara was beautiful enough. She was also intelligent. Once Dadou had had a bit of a weakness for intelligent women. Once, long ago, his world had stopped at three or four little things, and the beauty of a woman had been one of them. Then the word 'putrid' had dropped into his brain. His brain had corrupted his whole being. That corruption must be overcome. But how? He was beginning — and it was tragic — to non-exist. He told himself: 'Life is still there before you. All this will blow over, and you'll start again.' But 'all this' was becoming chronic. He was taking every fall in the world. He was going from one hell to another.

What made everything putrid was that it was tragic without being painful. Dadou needed pain. His body had become too silent, formed too much scar-tissue.

'Even if they do me in, let me at least be alive at the time. I'm going to fight. A dead man that fights is a fine thing in himself. A thing that fights is already . . . human.'

His throat went dry at the thought that the *Magistrate* might not have closed. The proprietress's smell came into his nostrils. He inhaled the cigarette smoke and the shots. And the corrupt side of the *Magistrate*, into which he had ventured one night — one only — without being able to go through with it: the bedrooms. He had paid. But the desire to have sex had abruptly left him. He had apologized to the girl, paid double, and gone back to the bar. He had filled the hole that his action had dug deep inside him with shots of alcohol. He had left the *Magistrate* around two in the morning. The streets had become more immense. People and things had all assumed fantastic dimensions that day; he had come close to believing in the world, in himself, in everything, even in God.

The following evening the governor helped him leave the prison, as planned. Time was like a virgin expanse before him. Yealdara came to meet him three streets from the army camp. They walked right through Bandal to reach her place. The world was just beginning. Dadou felt a craving for the *Magistrate*. A craving, too, for this tragic earth that his feet knew by heart.

'I've seen some people who might have helped us. Important people — four or five of them. They said that politically you're untouchable. You're a liability.'

'I've never had a political past,' Dadou said. 'How can I be a liability?'

'They said you're beyond help.'

Yealdara was living in a luxurious house right on the river, just outside Bandal. Dadou had no reason to wonder at the girl's wealth. There was her father, there was her sociology, and there were her years in Europe. She could have driven a Mercedes. She contented herself with a Datsun that bore a perfectly ordinary number-plate. The walls of the living-room were hung with photographs of Lumumba and one of Tabu-Ley.

'What are the papers saying?' Dadou asked.

'No one will know anything before the changeover. The governor is seeing to that.'

'When do we cross?'

'We must contact the fishermen first. But with your hair and that beard. . .'

'They're my insignia,' Dadou broke in.

'You're not a man. You're a thing. You don't think of other people. You don't see other people. You only see yourself.'

'That's right,' Dadou said. 'Coming into the world, though we're together sometimes, each of us has his own path. And I believe that for your own peace you must not give a damn about other people. You came as one, you will die as one, you must go through life as one. Needing others is a weakness if it's not just a delusion. I know, now, that I have never, in this whole vast world, had anyone but myself. And that is something that helps me a lot.'

Two big tears rolled silently down Yealdara's cheeks: 'You hard-hearted bastard!' But what love burned in her young heart! As Dadou spoke, each word hacked at her heart like an axe. 'This world of wounds!' he thought. 'This wounded earth!'

'There was a time when I wanted to love other people, listen to them, understand them, help them when they needed it. But that time is dead. The time passing through me today, the time alive in me today is wilderness time, the time of solitude. Don't cry. I'm talking about inside me. I'm talking to make a noise. Because squatting inside me is Fear with a capital F. But I admire you very much. You're a very exceptional girl. You are also beautiful.'

He was lying. He no longer believed in exceptional things. Yealdara's behaviour reached him in part, but did that matter? Those things were all dead as far as he was concerned. He scarcely remembered them. They slept together — on the bed, on the carpeted floor, in the grass. Sometimes she was in positions that made Dadou laugh. Sexual pleasure was something Dadou had left far, far behind. He went through the motions. But behind the motions all was emptiness, putridity, the desert of the flesh. One evening the drink in him whispered:

'If we have a child we'll call it Matty, or maybe Matta.'

'Matty doesn't mean anything.'

'It comes from mat. While we're doing it I'm thinking about my mat back there in prison.'

'I'm not giving you pleasure. . .'

'You are.'

She had burst into hiccupping sobs, her voice dying away in her pleasure. Her nostrils needed air, huge quantities of air. She was quivering like an old shred of newsprint in the wind. What world was she in? Dadou wondered. Next she was swept into a series of convulsions. Little by little the flesh sank back. For Dadou the whole thing had been nothing but warmth and a few noises: putridity. He had had a big enough heart once. With his wife. With the kid, too. He had lost it, though. Now he was trying to start again. But the emptiness — all around him?

'I'm mad, I'm mad,' he said again and again.

'Yes. But I want you to get well again,' Yealdara told him.

'Obliteration is the only thing that will cure me.'

'That's something you believe. You must obliterate the belief in order to free yourself from it.'

'I'm putting up a fierce fight. Do you believe that, at least — that I'm putting up a fierce fight?'

'I do, and I have hope.'

Again, Dadou was lying. He lacked the strength to fight. He was letting the world enter into him like a mouse entering its hole. She offered him beer and whisky. To this son of the *Magistrate*, however, beer was toads' piss. All it did was swell you up. Dadou wanted shots. Yealdara was incapable of giving him a shot with substance. That was something only men understood. Some men. She provided bed and board. The rest was there at the *Magistrate* in . . . what was the name of the street? How could he have forgotten the name of the street? Even the name of the proprietress. Four years and a few months. Even time could be forgotten. Buried. Poor girl, constantly being taken without feeling, like a glass of water.

'Try to get hold of a torch for me.'

'Tonight? I can't possibly.'

'Try.'

'What do you want to do?'

'Go and have a look at my place.'

'The house is a ruin.'

'I've a craving for that house. If you'd rather, give me a bit of money. I'll buy the torch on the way.'

They had nearly had an argument, but Yealdara had given in. Now Dadou was walking through the night. Some soldiers had stopped him for his papers, but these had been in order and he had quickly been released. He walked on, dreaming darkly. Twice he nearly got knocked down. He was haunted by the idea of not going back to Yealdara's house. But where else would he go? And why drive the girl to despair?

When he reached his neighbourhood, everyone was asleep. Dadou stole into the half-collapsed building, pushing doors open carefully: four years; dust and mildew. The front door, beaten down in the fighting that day, was still there. Dadou went straight to the bedroom. The bed was in place. Covered with dust and rubble. He threw himself down on it and slept deeply. The ceiling revealed a scrap of sky in which two stars swam. Dadou dreamed of the nights doused on that bed, nights well sunk in the savanna of time. He might have been a weed like the one growing on the roof, dipping with every breath of wind, because of that margin of friendship between the void and himself. He woke to find their photograph on the table, deep in dust. Only the eyes had withstood the passage of time.

'I'm a coward,' Dadou thought. 'The prince of cowards. Yet it's just as well. I've virtually denied the world, life, the lot. Simply because, when all's said and done, it takes my mind off things. All roads are closed before me. Yet I walk on. Like a coward. My particular cowardice, though, is a form of courage. I have denied all the world's road. And my walk is virginal. My heart — yes, there is my heart. But I've denied that, too. I have overcome myself. Overcome mediocracy. And all the mediocrats.'

Next day he decided to take a look at the *Magistrate*.

The town had changed a great deal: new street names, new squares, whole new districts. Dadou walked. Long hair was fashionable now, so that his own did not attract attention. The beard, however, made him look like a Communist or rather, as people here said, a left-wing revolutionary. And his gait, which was now quite clumsy, made people laugh — but also made them think. His dress aside, there was something of the West African about him. People here take their bearing very seriously. And to walk so clumsily the man must be from the other end of the continent: Senegal, Togo, Mali? Some country where people do not know how to walk.

It was as he had expected: the *Magistrate* had closed down. That kind of business never lasts long. Dadou staved off his thirst with insipid Belgian drinks. They make you drunk but do not insert you into the world. They fail to quicken the yearnings of the soul. They drown you, and that is all. Dadou had no desire to drown but wished, as before, to encounter Dadou, encounter the world, break through existence by doubling his weight. He walked for a long time, completely at random.

On the second occasion the people of the neighbourhood saw

him enter his house, but they took him for insane, and the insane are not prohibited from sheltering in ruins. Some children began to throw stones at him. He did not react, and they went away. They might have loved each other here, he thought, amid the dust and the debris, might have had the wind enter their bodies, hearts. Mice. Those mice again. Filthy brain-gnawers. Dadou watched them for a long time as they ran about the half-dark room. He remembered the drawer where they had kept their letters. Many of those letters had been tidied away there, intact, alive. Dadou gathered them all up and decided to return to Yealdara.

'I was beginning to worry.'

'That place is my home. It recharged me.'

'I know you aren't happy here.'

'It's not something you can understand. But I'm four years slow. I'm looking for myself. I have to look for myself. I met up with my smells back there. You cannot understand, but I'm a missing person.'

'Tell me, Dadou — did you love her?'

'Who?'

'Yavelde.'

Dadou went to her and pulled her against him. She was breathing fast. She was so frightened. Her skin swelled, her eyes dilated, her lips, her brow, her breasts grew larger. Dadou felt he had taken hell in his hands. What — not burning? What — so cold?

'Don't mention her to me ever again! Do you hear?'

'I want to know.'

'You cannot know what I don't know myself. I don't know what I wanted with her. She was too much for me. Nature was already so violent with me. But it was through her that it finished me off – I know that much. The rest. . .'

'*A mona nganga mpo na yo*,' Yealdara said in the vernacular.

'She bewitched you.'

'Oh, that stuff,' said Dadou.

'You have to believe in it sometimes.'

'Not me.'

'Come and look. I've made you a really good sauce. At least we can behave like a couple. We can get into habits: I can be content with some nice habits.'

'You're being unfair.'

'I want us, while we're waiting, to take the time to live and have dreams.'

The sauce was delicious. Dadou ate hungrily. Afterwards Yealdara handed him a little parcel.

'What is it?' Dadou asked.

'Open it,' she said. 'It's for the future.'

A little lead Christ. Dadou smiled.

'Ah, the Jew,' he said. 'Do you believe in him?'

'We all do. Even without wanting to.'

'Thank you, anyway,' Dadou said. 'I've nothing in particular against him, even if I no longer have the time to go to him.'

'He always has mercy.'

'I don't accept mercy, I'm not an object of pity. But let's talk about things that concern us now. I think it's right for me to cross the river. Have you any news of the governor?'

'Yes. He's waiting to hand over.'

'Still?'

'The fellow who was to relieve him has gone sick. We have to wait. It doesn't cost us anything to wait, does it? When we danced, that evening at the party, I thought I was being born again. I don't know how to say this. It was beautiful. It's still with me — here in my thighs, in my womb, under my dress, in my breasts, in my heart. That unaccountable thrill of the flesh. That unending joy. It's time that dies — I'm as before. But whatever we say about the heart, what the heart is only the heart knows.'

'The heart,' Dadou repeated. 'It's the heart that perhaps betrays us. All the rest of us is loyal. But I daren't say any more. Because all these words I keep bellowing — afterwards they're just holes inside me. Full of rats. Full of maggots. All these words. I daren't say any more. The heart. Yes, the heart — that's what bowls us over. The rest is obedient. The rest understands us, but not the heart. And then for some people, and to some extent for you, what I'm saying there is all just talk. But the things — they are my blood, my body, my life. I am talking to myself. I am telling myself. And it hurts dreadfully. I had two hearts, the first was broken, the second broke me. The result is. . . Listen — I am my friend, I keep nothing from myself, I tell myself everything. Basically the fact that you're there makes no difference to my monologue. I've happened, you can believe me there — I have taken place. Today all I am is this thing playing dead — a kind of nightmare. No, a nightmare cannot love other nightmares. Before I used to rely on time. But time is becoming impotent. Time no longer gets randy. And I'm panic-stricken. I'm going to die horizontal, with bits of me still alive.'

Yealdara had shed all her clothes and come to him. There was a satanic quality in her nudity that succeeded in rousing Dadou from his obsession. That harsh smell of lemon. That catfish smoothness. The honey on those lips. That milky substance.

'This will always make sense,' she said.

Dadou did not react. She went off to make him some coffee. That body: all silences and thrilling shapes. Dadou threw his heart and mind into it, but the flame would not catch. Dadou was sorry the *Magistrate* had closed. He thought of the delightful shots lying dormant somewhere in the neighbourhood. Insipid world of insipidities! One could never bring oneself to consume everything.

Yealdara put on a record while waiting for the coffee. She asked him to dance. They danced — two ebony nudes. They danced without either of them giving another thought to the coffee boiling dry in the saucepan.

'Poor coffee,' Dadou said.

'I didn't want you falling asleep. We have to keep busy. Otherwise, no Matty! What do we do if it's a boy?'

'Don't talk about it.'

'But I want us to talk. It'll be a long night if we don't.'

'All my nights are long,' Dadou said. 'I like them long.'

A car came to a halt outside. A horn blared, and Yealdara moved to open the door. Dadou stopped her.

'Don't go out like that. And wait till I'm out of sight — it might be them.'

Dadou looked around for a safe place to hide. He slipped down behind the settee.

'Not there,' Yealdara said. 'Get in the laundry basket.'

The horn blared again. She ran out, straightening her nightdress as she went. The man stayed behind the wheel. In the darkness Yealdara recognized the governor.

'Aren't you coming in?'

'No.'

'Is something wrong?'

'Something's wrong. Tell him to slip away tomorrow. Things have reached breaking-point. The frontiers may be closed. Relations have broken down between the other bank and us. Their Cabinet meets tomorrow. Afterwards you know how they act. Lose no time. Be extra careful.'

The car roared off into the night with no lights showing. Yealdara was left trembling in every limb. It was not to last. It was not made to last. It was too vulnerable. Too beautiful, too.

'Who was it?' Dadou asked, climbing out of the laundry.

'The governor. He says you must leave tomorrow.'

'Try your coffee again. It will be a long night.'

11

'This night — this vast night. Everything around me is noble. Everything is great. My heart, too, grows great and turns back, as it used to, towards you. I am thinking of all our nights, our time, our loves. I love you. I feel it here, in all my flesh, in all my blood, and on everything I touch. It is as if you were here with me. And man's time were chiming with God's time. In my heart, deeper than my mind, all is jostling movement. And all, alas, off balance.

What do you expect, my darling man? Such is life. A burden, still. So are words. But what matters to me now is what sleeps beneath the words, not the words themselves; what matters is what there is beneath things, not the things themselves; what there is beneath lives. But it may be my body is mistaken. Now, darling, I shall never be sure of anything any more. Time — ah, coarse man's time in the shadow of God's time! I shall not even be sure of time any more. My heart has crushed me. And in me time no longer germinates. I was alive, more alive than life. Words. You don't understand all these words. You gulp them down raw. Maybe you fall for them — here I, as I used to do, become swollen with our existence. With the world, too. This, as it used to be, is the inauguration. Old body, of course, old habits. But young hope. Young obstinacy. I have grown to your height, grown up to our lovemaking, and caught up in our kisses I watch, I witness the birth of a sweet transgression. I am flinty, stony, rocky with our ancient presence. But these words — it's as if there were no longer anything beneath them. Beneath anything, for that matter.

'In me the flesh is new, the old skin is shed. My blood, too, is new. My breath, my eyes, my cries, the bite of my heart. I remember: the night, our lovemaking, time. Even if this time is afraid. I love you. Maybe you know that. But have you ever believed it? You judge me. By my heart of stone. My cavernous temperament. Darling! We were the womb of the world, the matrix of time. But, oh!

'This night gushing up in my flesh is the least absurd in the world. The most reliable of my life. The least human, too. It is swallowing my heart. The heart dances beneath man, beneath the body, beneath the whole world, beneath habits and hopes — but after the heart comes nothingness. You won't understand all these words. Unless you read them all your life. Really they're words of blood. Stark. . . Heart-words.

'I have pangs as they leave me — as if I had given birth to twins. Yes, darling. They are seed-words. They are planted. Waited on. They germinate. They will flower and bear fruit. Words of life. I recall our nights in the other time. The starkest there have ever been. Our sounds. The bed an altar, all the sheets a snare. Our smells. The deep places. Your deep place, too. I remember the bedclothes. I was right to leave. I love you. This thing matters more than my life. The words, though. In this time, at this time, there is nothing left beneath the words. Tonight I went outside to look at the stars. Strangely, they appeared to me in pairs, all bearing our marks. They convinced me that we were great. But that we are past! I came back to this bed, our altar, our temple. Believe it or not, I cried. Once again I ventured my body on that former time, on things already said, on that time when I was happy without quite realizing, mother of the world without knowing it. Would we have realized that a kiss, an embrace, a smile — that they were worlds? Worlds of our own in this world of other people. Time has outlived us. I regard happiness as man's first duty on this earth, and I am still the same unchanging candidate for happiness. . .'

He could read no further. His heart had stirred within him like an ancient giant. His blood felt as if it was about to fail him. So did his flesh. By what road had he contrived to leave that world? To arrive at nothing but this putridity? He had said goodbye to himself. Very dramatic. And all roads were dead. Those that came into him, and those that went out from him. The outside was dead. Sealed like a box. And Dadou was putting up a fierce fight. The inside, too, had begun to cave in. He was being smothered. A gradual encirclement.

The letter — the first in the pile he had dared to read — was one she had written years before. It dated from those troubled times when great loves cross the bridge of realities. And the other bank brings storms, paroxysms, blood. She had packed her bags and moved in with her mother in Kimbanseke Street. And he, Dadou, had taken the path of solitude. That had been when the encirclement began; he recalled their argument, a perfect torrent of abuse.

'You can go and sleep with him — go ahead . . . go ahead. . .'

He had torn up all their photographs, even those of their wedding. Oh, that face that came to haunt him!

Dadou destroyed the letter. Yealdara, meanwhile, talked

virtually to herself. It was a very long night.

'You'll be able to breathe. There's plenty of air over there — clean air. There's the Great South Road. At the fishing village you're to ask for Fortuné Loupanzo, an old man also known as Sacramento. In fact better known by that name than by the other. If he's got my letter, you'll have your meal ticket.'

They set out at five, the Datsun running smoothly and quietly. Dadou thought about his cell-mate. Falodiati had got out two years before him. An escape. He must be over there in some fishing village, spending his time guzzling fish. Dadou also thought of the night preceding the escape, when he had pinched Falodiati's nostrils to stop him snoring like a diesel engine. Unsuccessfully, though: he had gone on snoring. In fact it had been like that every night. For two years. Dadou keeping vigil over his swine of a friend. In the morning the latter had revealed his plan: during working time he would give the warders the slip and get across the river. If he did not return in the evening, that would mean the plan had worked. He had not returned. It had never occurred to Dadou to leave like that. He was expecting to win his case. Anyway, who would have taken him out on work shift? He was a special prisoner.

'I'll come over if you get established.'

Dadou shrugged his shoulders. A group of soldiers was marching towards them. Yealdara braked suddenly: she had not seen them. The soldiers asked for their papers, which Dadou handed over in a pile. They counted the cards and the coloured dockets. They were all there.

'Thank you, citizens.'

Yealdara drove off again, following the riverbank. Bands of mist hung in the headlights. What a bloody awful country, Dadou thought. A man could not even bring himself to hate it. They were below Devil's Island now. Down where the bloody town met the country and tiny fishing villages grew up like dreams in the scrub, huts grouped in twos and threes, their walls cluttered with curious contraptions that man had spent years inventing and with which he hunted fish. Canoes could already be seen tracing silvery wakes over the khaki expanse of the river. Dadou took out a letter. There was not enough light. He put it back into his pocket. Birds were flitting from grass-stem to grass-stem, from bush to bush. Then they were on sand, in the world of fish and fishing. The smell of the river. The bitter smell of fresh blood and the ceaseless khaki flow beneath the aquatic plants. The Datsun would go no farther. Damned Japanese cars!

Yealdara took the bag of food and walked ahead of him, down to the water's edge. Day was already breaking. A grey day. Downstream some smugglers were unloading a Toyota. It was well past their time, and the lateness amplified all their movements. On the other side many products had become worth their weight in gold. People were not slow to take advantage. It was called 'profit-fishing', and those who did it were known as 'Leo's idle work-force.' Independence had come and there was no longer a Leopoldville, but the name had stuck. To tease one another people still talked about 'French Congo' or 'Belgian Congo' or 'Portuguese Angola'.

A group of fishermen came up to them, smelling of rags and tobacco and fish. The oldest one was smiling wryly. Yealdara held out her hand to him.

'You want to go across?' the old man asked.

'He does.'

'It's tough over there.'

'Not just over there.'

'Here you can still breathe,' said the old man.

'Over there you're up to your ears in Chinese,' said the youngest member of the group. 'Your own son asks you for your papers before you can step on the patch. Your wife wants to see your papers when you get into bed.'

The old man broke into a laugh that the youngster awkwardly prolonged. He rummaged in his pockets and brought out a lump of tobacco, which he proceeded to chew together with a quarter of a cola nut. Dadou held out his hand. The old man, understanding, slipped a piece of cola into it.

'Have you got your papers, at least?'

'Yes,' said Dadou.

'Going over on business?'

'No.'

'If it's a political one we're not too keen. They're shooting people like rabbits.'

'It's an ordinary one,' Yealdara said.

'So why aren't you using the ordinary route? Where are your papers?'

The old man held the papers to his nose and took a long sniff. He smiled knowingly.

'Not very old, these papers,' he said.

'He's had them a year.'

'Doesn't smell like it. A couple of months. Not even that. When you go on the water, girl, you've got to tell the truth. Lying makes the river angry. How long?'

'A few days,' Dadou said.

'What sort of a deal did you say this was?'

'I've escaped from prison.'

'Ah! And how did you get into prison?'

'The way everyone does.'

'How's that?'

'It's a long story.'

'Tell it or we alert the frontier.'

'*Tangala, Tangala buki e! ku buaku ko eh! nkala muisi mamba! Tangala, Tangala buki ee! Eh! nsi na bwa e!*'

It was the song of the crab's walk, and the young fisherman sang it wonderfully well. It was also a statement heavy with menace. 'May I fall, crab, son of the water, walk, walk and "crab", but don't you fall, son of the water.' Briefly, Dadou told his story. The old man chewed a lump of tobacco. The cola was finished.

'All right, but since we're taking a risk . . . it'll cost more.'
'How much?' Yealdara asked.

'It's prison, you see, girl. But we'll do you this one because you're my children. And if you refuse we alert the frontier.'

The old man meant it. His eyes were knowing. Dadou, staring fixedly at the opposite bank, found the smell of his rags distracting. All he saw was Yealdara handing the old man a wad of notes and the old man counting them with a broad smile. His departure was paid for. Now he must face the khaki fury of the river. But the old man inspired confidence. Departure, then. . . Leaving everything. Dadou was leaving nothing. The shots, possibly. The *Magistrate* was dead, as was all the rest: everything was dead here, only he was still alive. The path of man is pain indeed. Dadou, however, had suffered beyond pain. 'Majestic river!' he thought. 'We call you Congo. We call you Zaïre, but you — what do you call us? How do you see us, how do you think of us?' The khaki-coloured waves swelled Dadou's heart. They distended his flesh and stirred his insides.

For the space of a moment he yearned to be a river. Once over there, if time allowed, he would drink, he would dance. If his papers worked, if they stood up to scrutiny over there, he meant to make every effort to live.

Yealdara's heart was heavy, her lovely face convulsed with emotion.

'If they don't close the frontier I'll come in a few days.'

'They'll be closing it,' the old man said. 'The situation's tense between them and us.'

Yealdara hung her arms around Dadou's neck. She kissed him on the mouth. The fishermen exchanged meaning glances. 'The white man's ways are here to stay,' thought the old man. 'The ancestors will never be right again on this earth. At partings she gave you a tuft of hair or some intimate object. But not her saliva. Blood, yes. Sometimes there were two bleedings.

You mixed the blood and then drank the mixture. Those most in love touched each other's private parts. The more sensitive wept, mingling their tears. But not insipid saliva!'

Yealdara had remained on the bank for a long time, waving one hand above her head. She had caught the dimensions of a beautiful dream. As the canoe neared the middle of the river she melted and dissolved in the pure air of early morning. As if she had not existed. Dadou thought of the cemetery with its crosses. Iron crosses and wooden crosses — iron ones for the rich and fortunate, wooden ones for the poor. When the government did the burying, though, the cross was sometimes forgotten. Well, you know. . . Governments are always forgetting things. And since no one had been there to do the reminding, Dadou did not even expect there to be a wooden cross for his little devils.

The smell and turbulence of the water came close to reviving a body that had lived a hundred lives. It sang, the water; it seemed to be making a promise. But what can anyone promise a human stump but limbs with which to make an effort? That he would do. He would make every effort. Even just for a shot of leaf spirit.

He rummaged in his little wrist bag and took out a fresh letter. Some letters and a few old photographs were all he had in the world now. And his papers. But it was over there that his papers would. . . It was over there that his papers would start to mean something again.

'My darling,
I have received your violent words. Cruel words? Yes, there has been this short stretch when my own flesh melted over me, threatening to crush me. There is this hole between us — in time, in hope, in our whole bodies. In all my words, too. It was your fault: you stopped responding to our flings, our precious illusions of youth. We were still young. But you

were not on our scale any more. You spent every night and every morning working for your diplomas. You abandoned me to what I am: this terrible cry of flesh. You delivered me up to this nervy drop of matter that I am by extinguishing all the dreams around me. Hence the hole: you'd made my entire body come up into my mouth, choking me. So I cried out. That's a beautiful thing — a woman crying out. I went with the Belgian. To make my cry seem more sordid to me. Ah, what a life we had before us, around us, behind us! If, now, you can understand, forgive, forget. . .'

Dadou had wanted to and had tried. But forgiveness, in matters of the body, in matters of the heart, cannot be fabricated. Even forgetting is hell. She had come back. But she smelled of the Belgian. A powerful, stubborn smell. And when they were between the sheets he used to see Belgians with their uncircumcized cocks. That roused him. So he banged very hard in order to forget. Too hard. The whole neighbourhood had tried to court her. The street saw her as a pushover. So how many others were banging away like him? And who was the best fucker of the bunch? Who delivered the biggest bang? Who was the master fucker? Whether or not it was him made no difference. But the one word 'bunch' had ruined everything.

Yes, there had been that neglect, that slovenliness in sexual matters when Dadou was reading for his doctorate. Diplomas and bed do not go together.

'. . . Do you know, darling? I often say to myself: I didn't deceive him; at least I didn't deceive him. But all that is mere words. And behind the words there's me. With my lapse. My sullied body. And I spit. Basically that's all I was ever trying to do: spit. I realized what a hell my body had become for you, for us, and I left. I left, but I'm not finished.'

Water came into his eyes. Riverwater, but also the water of his own body. Suicide, Dadou thought. Yes, there were all those crabs and fish. There would be the voyage among the stones. Then the return to the surface. And the flies. And the stink. There was the meeting of the waters. But suicide. . .

The bank stood out sharply before his eyes. Territories extended from one side of this river to the other. Peoples, too, with their customs and their doings. A party had come down to meet them. Half a dozen hard-muscled men helped them to moor the canoe. There was an exchange of passwords to find out whether the authorities were watching the river. The fishermen's code.

'We're just fishermen,' one of them offered. 'The crocodile has not left the river. How about over there?'

'The waters of the river are white,' the old man replied. 'Are you going across?'

'Yes.'

'With sticky stuff?'

'Not altogether. We're in order, but with those fellows. . . Best to know which way they're looking. What about you? Have you brought something?'

'Yes.'

'Political?'

'No. This one's personal.'

'Know anyone here?'

'I don't know,' said the old man. 'You can ask him yourself. We've done our bit.'

'Has he got papers, at least?'

'Ah, a black man's cleverer than his papers, you know. He'll always have them.'

'Right,' the man on the bank breathed. 'Fine.'

'Right, fine,' echoed the old man.

'If he's smart he'll be all right. And if things get sticky, which it looks as if they're going to. . .'

'In what way?'

'Politics, as usual. There may be a coup. Tomorrow, or at any rate by Tuesday.'

'Power,' the old man sighed.

'That's right, power. What won't it get up to here. But we don't give a damn. As long as they leave us the river!'

The old man motioned to Dadou to disembark. His smile, his malicious manner, even his look reminded Dadou of all the fishermen he had ever seen. But here they fished for everything.

'You'll find some people in that hut over there,' said one of the fishermen on the new bank. 'We've got other things to do. And we'd better be quick about it. If things get sticky they'll close the river, and we don't want that to happen while we're on the water. They're a bad lot, you know, those fellows!'

'Things seem quiet enough here, though.'

'Huh!'

The old man shook hands with all the fishermen. Then he asked Dadou to move on. The earth here was peaceful, swollen with sunshine and silence beside the river wrestling with its brute waters. The earth was listening. So was the grass. Here and there large stones stood like dreamy scholars, staring at the river. They were the beginning of the Plateau of the Cataracts.

In the hut an old woman and two youngsters were preparing fish for smoking. It must have been eight o'clock. Dadou found himself being offered the traditional fishermen's soup. He was not very hungry, but he remembered the proverb: 'Eat in the morning and you will not yawn at the funeral.' He stuffed himself with fish, vegetables, and roots.

'You've come at a bad time,' the old woman said. 'It looks as if things are about to get sticky in town. Here coups have become almost a . . . almost. . .'

She searched for the word but failed to find it. Dadou smiled at her, though it was not a full smile. The old woman smiled back, showing repulsively long teeth.

'Where do you want to go?' she asked.

'I don't know.'

'No!' she exclaimed, adding: 'Here you have to know.'

'I'll know,' Dadou said.

'Are you familiar with the country?'

'No,' Dadou told her.

'So how do you presume to imagine you'll know?'

'I will,' said Dadou.

The old fisherman came to say goodbye, bringing the little wrist bag that Dadou had left in the canoe. Dadou remembered that among the letters and banknotes there was a slip of paper on which Yealdara had jotted the name of a fisherman. He rummaged in the bag and brought it out.

'Do you know a man called Fortuné, also known as Sacramento?' he asked the old woman.

'Yes. He's a neighbour of ours. Or should I say he was. . .'

'Was?' Dadou asked.

'They came and arrested him yesterday morning. His wife and children were able to get away. He was not warned and ran straight into them. They beat him so badly we wonder if he's still alive.'

'What was he charged with?'

'Huh!' the old woman snorted. 'Here you can be charged with the way you walk, even. This country's the limit, you know.'

'Everywhere's the limit,' Dadou told her. 'It makes me laugh, all the talk of white minorities when the whole of Africa is teeming with black minorities.'

'Don't say things like that, please. People might think we were talking politics.'

The old woman was of an attractively solid build. But for the scattering of white glitter in her hair she could have passed for half her age.

'Here we only talk politics at meetings. At any other time it's called rebellion and is severely punished.'

'This is the first time I've talked about such things,' Dadou said.

'Well, here we don't talk about them,' the old woman insisted.

'It's like that everywhere,' said Dadou. 'Everywhere.'

'What we talk about here is the river and fish. Beyond that, beyond the river and fish, it's prison. Have you ever been to prison? I have. For some days. They were looking for a fugitive. They picked on us. For a fortnight we were treated like fish — not even that well.'

Dadou looked at the old woman with admiration. She has managed to come back from prison intact. She is brave. Not you. Thousands have gone away. And come back. In good shape. They have started again. Besides, for you prison only came afterwards — you've got over prison. What threw you was what had gone before. But you can do it: you can make the effort. You have to. Really try and make every effort.

'Fortuné is our neighbour. We owe it to him to let you stay. And if things get sticky we can even take the odd risk. How did you meet him?'

'I don't know him. A girlfriend told me about him. A girl called Yealdara.'

'Ah, that one! She came here two or three times for the holidays as a kid. She'll be grown-up now. You must be. . . Never mind — what does it matter! Just the name, Yealdara, will get you everything here. You'll see. Even if things do turn sticky everyone will protect you. Ah, that one! When she came this whole little village was in love with her. What's she doing on the other side? She used to say she'd become a doctor and return to look after us all.'

'She did sociology.'

'And what's she been doing since?'

'Thinking.'

'No! And why didn't she do medicine?'

'I don't know.'

'She's betrayed this whole village. We adored her. She's let us down. She deserves every curse there is.'

The old woman's face had turned bitter. Dadou no longer dared look at her. He felt a longing for his letters. But there was not enough light in the room to read by. He confined himself to the photographs, which he pored over one by one, forgetting the old woman.

'The land of monologues,' she said. 'What's your name?'

'Dadou.'

'Is that your first name?'

'I'm from Zaïre.'

'Ah, yes, of course. How old are you?'

'I can't remember.'

'I had two sons like you. They were twins. They were killed at the radio station, defending the cause. The cause! What am I supposed to make of the cause? The cause takes no account of the heart. Nor of mothers. It takes away your two boys. They get a street named after them, or a square. And that's as far as it goes. Afterwards everything becomes the cause. And if you knew what the cause can do in a mother's insides, right at the spot where pain sleeps. It moves. It stirs. It wounds.'

The two youngsters had finished their work. They were listening to the old woman with close attention. From time to time they threw a furtive glance at the stranger. Their way of opening their eyes suggested that in spite of their youth they had lived. They had seen things. One of them addressed the old woman.

'Grandmother, if the gentleman went to the capital someone could help him. . .'

'The gentleman stays here,' the old woman interjected. 'You will both help him here.'

'There's room on the mat for two,' the younger one said. 'On the mat and in the canoe. When grandfather died he said: "We must love those who suffer." '

'Yes.' The old woman nodded approvingly. 'He said that.

You will both love Mr Dadou. You'll take him fishing.'

'Has he got his papers?' the younger one asked.

'You can't cross the river without papers,' said the old woman.

She looked lovingly at the two children. One of them had fish-scales in his hair. The old woman removed them one by one. They were fine boys, innocent, clear-faced, stout-hearted. One was called Sylvain and the other Henri. Henri, the younger of the two, wanted to take Dadou to the river there and then.

'You're not to go out,' the old woman ordered. 'Things may get sticky. When people from the town come picking on fishermen, something's up.'

Around three or four o'clock Dadou went and lay by the river, his eyes fixed on the opposite bank. A girl came down to fetch water. She stopped and looked at the long-haired stranger for some minutes. She smiled at him. But Dadou was still dreaming. The girl went up to him. Ah, those riverside girls! They have their own ways. They may even take the initiative. Behaviour one would not expect from hill girls. It is as if the contact with water induced a dizziness of the flesh. As if the river compelled passion.

'You look devastated,' she told him.

Dadou did not respond. All that khaki-coloured water was filling and swelling his heart. Distending his body. The road ahead of him was dead. He was determined, as he kept saying to himself, to make every effort.

'Are you not from here?'

'No,' Dadou said.

'That's a powerful river.'

'Yes, it is.'

'My name's Rita.'

'And my name is Dadou. I'm from the other side.'

'What's it like over there?'

'I don't know.'

The girl filled her basin and pulled it back to the bank. The water was full of grains of sand and little bits of weed. Dadou looked up and was struck by the strange resemblance Rita bore to Yavelde. He rubbed his eyes. He rubbed his heart against the sand. Rita had Yavelde's nose, her mouth, even her eyes. She had her forehead and her smile. All the alcohol Dadou had ever swallowed came awake in his head. 'Every effort,' he thought. He started to move away.

'Don't go,' she said. 'You can help me lift the basin.'

She sat there in her top and bikini briefs. Dadou dared not look at her. How stupid it is, man's heart! How stupid its throbbing; how stupid its progress through the world. For the first time for years Dadou was afraid of his heart, of his faculties, of the way ahead, of life. Rita swam like a bronze vision in the raging waters of the Congo. They called the river the Congo here, the Zaïre over there. But all that was the result of man's foolishness.

She threw water at him, and it reached his heart. Dadou gazed at the mysterious body conveying him back to the surface of the world and of life, laughing, transcending the limits of bodies to fan out in dreams. She came and sat beside him. 'I was killed back there on the other bank.' Had he really heard the words? 'I was killed. . .'

'What do you do in life?' she asked.

'Nothing,' Dadou replied. 'And you?'

'I'm in the Party.'

'What do you do in the Party?'

'Fight.'

'You're lucky.'

She was bursting with enthusiasm. With beauty, too. A carnal shot such as Dadou had not had for years. She inebriated him. And everything around him had turned liquid: stones, trees, huts, sky, the two riverbanks. Everything was melting, merging. The first shot in the world, imbibed from a glass called Rita. The first resurrection. The first road back. A few weeks' resurrection.

'Where do you live?'

'In a little village. Not far from here. We're thinking about the Congress. And you?'

'I'm staying with the fishermen. I'm in hiding.'

'For political reasons?'

'No, fate. What's the little village called?'

'If I have a moment I'll pop over to the fishing village and say hello.'

She had gone. Time had passed. Dadou had waited: two months, three. Rita had not come back.

He asked Henri where the Party village might be.

'What would a fisherman want with the Party village? That kind of thing is no concern of ours. They built about twenty special huts a couple of kilometres from here, guarded by soldiers. You're a fisherman — what do you want to go there for?'

'Show me the way,' said Dadou.

'Why do you want to know the way to hell?'

'I know a demon.'

'The Party's holiday season is over. All you'll find there now is soldiers. All the demons have gone. There's a time when you meet the loveliest women in the country there, when the leaders come for their break. You hear the best bands there, too.'

Dadou was folding up the mat on which he and Henri slept. The old woman was preparing the fish soup. Sylvain was sleeping with neighbours and had not yet arrived.

'Dadou says he's got a friend at the Party village.'

'No!' the old woman exclaimed.

She came over and took him by the shoulders. Her face was suddenly racked by deep, taut, sad wrinkles as panic etched itself into her old body. She was almost trembling.

'What have you done? The Party village is the fishermen's hell. How did you get there?'

'I haven't been there,' Dadou said. 'I have a girlfriend there.'

The old woman looked at him in amazement. For a moment she was speechless.

'If you tell them that in the village here they'll tie a big stone round your neck and throw you into the middle of the river. That place is the way to mourning and desolation. Oh, we ought to have told you the story! Three years ago some people came from across the river and attacked that village. They massacred the peaceable holiday-makers and then left again in their canoes. It was a terrible thing. The government got excited and decided to take revenge on the fishermen. That was when I lost my poor husband. Everyone here lost someone. After the funerals, at night time, all the fishermen from round about met together. A man talked to them — someone from Chad called Nangadoumbaye. He said very little, but he ended up with this: "May all the demons of the river and all its curses remain with that village until the end of time." After him Mbia from Cameroon said something. He too put a curse on the Party village.'

They loved God in this part of the country. He had provided the river. The river provided life. Life provided all the rest. It was the bridge between the present day and the ancestors. It offered the joy of killing a fish. There were many fishermen. From every part of the continent, facing the water, the stones, the heavy mud where the hyacinth grew.

There were even some Portuguese: three couples. The only whites. They manufactured salt fish. They did not go on the river much, whereas the others went out in their little boats for weeks, sometimes for months on end. For the rest, though, they lived the life of the other fishermen. And they would undoubtedly die their death. One day.

12

They had given him a good beating and thrown him down on the riverbank. They might have pushed him a bit farther and that would have been that. The world would have been at an end for him. But they had left him there in the mud and the leaves that in the language of these parts they call 'New Congo'. His body felt as heavy as that of an old dead fish. He tried to move his limbs one by one. Just. Nothing broken, possibly. His eyes could see no more than a little veil of light, a torn veil of red shadows with flies weaving in and out of them.

The old woman and Sylvain had been in town for two days. Henri and many of Dadou's friends were on the river. He had been unable to go: soldiers were patrolling the river because of the incidents in July. Makaya, who had never liked Dadou, had taken the opportunity to rouse the village against him.

'If the soldiers decide to search the huts they'll find him. And if they find a suspicious person in our huts, it will be the worse for us. We don't want a lousy stranger causing our children, our wives, and our own selves to run risks extending to the possible loss of our lives. We don't want an idiot who can't even fish to. . .'

It had been a lengthy speech. The crowd could not make up its mind. People liked the foreigner. But Makaya was right: if the soldiers came they would take him for a member of the Resistance. And a village that sheltered members of the Resistance could expect no mercy. They would set fire to it. All the inhabitants would be driven away, perhaps killed. Prevention was better than cure, so a group of men hostile to Dadou had gone to the old woman's hut after nightfall. They were torn between two solutions: calling in the soldiers, or taking him down to the river. The river was better. Because the foreigner might talk, might admit that he had been there for months. The soldiers would fail to understand why the villagers had moved so slowly. The Party needed militants who were prompt, not such sluggards. Here was a man with the look of an enemy of the people. So they had taken him out. They had dragged him down to the river. And there, in a slimy pool, they had beaten him and left him for dead.

Henri went looking for him the morning he returned to the village. He had brought back lots of fish: Dadou would help him smoke them. He asked all the neighbours. No one gave him a proper answer. A foreigner, some said, might just leave as he had come. No, Henri thought, *he* could never leave like that, without a word. He was not that sort. He had reached the stage of sharing all his thoughts and all his secrets with his beloved Henri. He had even told him about Makaya's daughter and how she had made amorous advances to him. And about Widow Nabadunali, who had taken to hanging around him. If he had decided to leave, Henri would have known. So he went on looking — for three days and three nights.

Old Ambami whispered a few words to him about Makaya's

intrigue. 'They were planning to make him disappear in order
to save the village,' she said.

'And did they?'

'It looks like it.'

'Did they throw him in the river? A curse on them all if
they. . .'

'Yes, a curse on them all. They do not know the sacred laws
of hospitality. If that is what they did, one day the ants will eat
up their flesh. Flies will lay eggs in their mouths.'

Dadou, asleep, thought he could see hands of light descending
to touch his forehead. Slowly he opened his eyes.

'Why did they do that?' he asked. He spoke mechanically,
repeating his question three times.

Unable to lift him because of his weight, Henri dragged him
through the mud and over the sand to his canoe.

'Why did they do that?' Dadou asked again.

Henri said nothing. He was paddling briskly. Behind the
point of Devil's Island the sun was setting in bands of gold
licked with copper and silver flames. The river was lit like one
long, sliding fire, oily and exhilarating. An image of the
difference between the nobility of things and human ugliness.

'Why did they do that?' Dadou asked in his delirium.

And the canoe forged on through the fires of evening.

'God,' Henri breathed, 'why did you create men? There
would be the river. There would be the clay and the fish. And
there would be silence and peace. Love and harmony.'

'There'd be no love,' came the whisper from a corner of his
mind. And Henri said aloud:

'There'd be no love.'

And that would be regrettable, because it is love that moves
and stirs and quickens matter.

He looked at Dadou with love and admiration. Where did

this man come from? Where was he going? Who was he, really? The village had come into view. Its shadows, its huts, its trees. Henri began to curse everything. In their cowardice they had stooped to throwing a man to the flies, without trial, without scruple, without pity. Some women and children were washing themselves in the river where Henri usually moored his canoe. The vessel drove straight at the bathers, who were forced to scatter, jostling one another like an army in flight. Curses filled the air.

'Are you mad or something?' came an elderly woman's voice.

Henri did not reply. He tied up his canoe and pulled Dadou to the bank.

'Why did they do that?'

Two women stepped forward from the crowd of bathers to give him a hand.

'What's up?'

'How did it happen?'

He was bombarded with questions. But Henri did not reply. What should he say to them? Some of them knew all about it. It could not be otherwise.

The wounded man was carried to the centre of the village. People gathered round, there were questions, murmurings, little groups formed. Various versions of the story emerged, some stating that the foreigner had been attacked by a group of soldiers, that he had held them off for a while, wounding or killing a number of them. . . Radio Baobab.

Makaya put about a gloomier version. According to him the foreigner was trafficking in precious stones. He had been molested by the frontier police. And since those fellows always needed stones more than they needed people, they had left him on the riverbank, half-dead. For most of the villagers, however, Dadou became the hero of a legend already taking shape in their minds. They began likening him to Lukeni, the famous founder of the kingdom of Congo. Henri thrust aside those who were standing round the wounded man and began to thunder:

'We are a village of cowards. All we shall bring forth in future will be fear and cowardice. This man has done nothing to us. Yet we give him this cowardly beating. A beating so bad he is now blind in one eye. We have torn his flesh with our teeth, we sons of fear. May God curse us! May the river and the ancestors curse us!'

There were more murmurings in the crowd, yet other versions.

'I say again: our father is cowardice and our mother fear. We have forgotten the most elementary laws of hospitality.'

The crowd began shouting on Dadou's behalf, but its anger found no butt. Makaya and his cronies were shouting too, so that there was now no seeing who could have carried out the attack.

'No,' Makaya cried in ear-splitting tones. 'The man is not wanted here, but he shouldn't have been treated like that. It's disgusting!'

'When he can talk,' roared others, 'we'll ask him to say who attacked him.'

'If anyone dares come near him again with any evil ideas,' Henri bellowed, 'he shall die for all the ones who started this. Truly this is the home of crime and cowardice, this is the home of treason. But the next man who tries anything I shall kill with my own hands. And I shall feed his carcass to the dogs.'

'*Olum' a niama*,' someone called out. 'Son of a man.'

The phrase went to Henri's head so that, bold beyond prudence, he loosed off a few filthy words about soldiers. Have a care, my friend!

His long speech over, Henri got two girls who were very fond of Dadou to help him install his friend in the old woman's hut. Between moans the patient mumbled deliriously. 'What a putrid thing to do,' he said over and over again, or 'Why did they do that?' Henri cooked him a fish and tried to feed it to him. It was all he could do to swallow a few spoonfuls of soup. His throat was nearly lifeless. To raise him off the hard ground

Henri had laid banana leaves beneath his mat.

Next day his condition worsened. From time to time he lost consciousness. The two girls — the only people Henri allowed into the hut — wept at his bedside. Henri himself endeavoured to remain calm and confident.

'If he dies, we won't even know where he came from.'

'Across the river,' the other girl said.

'Across the river is a big place.'

'He has lovely eyes, a lovely nose, a lovely mouth. Unusual on a man, a mouth like that.'

'Rita!' Dadou said, coming out of his coma. 'Yavelde . . . Yealdara!'

He fell asleep again. The girls summoned Henri, who was mending nets outside. He came in and rushed over to the dying man.

'Has . . . has he gone?'

He felt the heart. Its weak beat was growing progressively weaker.

'We must call a doctor.'

'He has no safe papers,' Henri said.

'At least he'll get treatment before they arrest him.'

'Not necessarily. They've arrested people who were dead.'

'There's a pygmy fisherman in the village. He knows lots of plants.'

'Fetch him,' Henri said. 'But hurry!'

The sick man had started to hiccup. His body was momentarily shaken by violent convulsions. Why must a man die without even knowing he is dying? Without anyone around him really knowing?

Henri began to think about his father, about the many members of his family whom time or the country had swallowed up. He thought of his mother and Sylvain. Why were they not back yet? When the law slips from the grasp of those who control it, it becomes a matchless killing machine. And here the law had indeed begun to run wild: killing, wounding, fleecing. Why were those two. . .?

Dadou's chest tilted up, his head went back. But his breath kept coming. It just would not let go. Three days Henri and the two girls spent waiting for it to let go. But it kept coming. On the evening of the third day Sylvain and the old woman returned from the town.

'Why did they do that?' the old woman cried after hearing the story.

'In this place,' the younger of the two girls said, 'they do nothing else. When a country has gone mad, the things people do make you wonder.'

The old woman quickly prepared several strange mixtures, moistening the sick man's lips with them. She cut his tongue and rubbed obscure powders into the cuts. Life was still stirring in the great body as it slipped into silence and immobility.

Next morning a long line of soldiers turned up at the village. They started searching the huts at the opposite end of the village to where the old woman's hut stood. Their commanding officer, a sergeant with an enormous paunch, directed the operation as he intimidated the villagers with his AK. Fishermen are always afraid of a rifle.

'Once a soldier, always a soldier,' Henri breathed.

'What will we do if. . .?'

'We'll explain.'

'What explaining can you do to a soldier?'

'They can't take him away. He'll be dead before he's gone a hundred yards. . . Let them come and get him if he recovers. Until then they have to. . .'

'They'll take him away,' Sylvain said.

'I'll defend him even if they. . .'

'You're not going to play the fool for a man who's already dead.'

Dadou moved his lips. No doubt he was still saying his 'Why did they do that?' Henri, Sylvain, the two girls, and the old woman all craved these movements, keeping constant watch on his mouth, his eyes, his rib-cage, fearful lest death had already taken up residence there for ever.

'Lord God,' the old woman breathed, 'do your bit. We have done ours.'

'There are some countries in the world God can no longer reach,' Henri said.

'Let him speak from far off,' the old woman insisted.

The soldiers were going through the hut next door. If they were searching like this it was because someone had tipped them off. In which case they knew where. . . And the rest of it was just for effect.

The invincible 'here'! Henri thought. The land of shams! The land of pregnancies. The land of paper.

'Papers?'

The two girls, Henri, Sylvain, and the old woman presented their bunches of cards. They were all there.

'What about his?'

'That's someone we fished out of the river half-drowned,' Henri lied.

'We live in troubled times,' the sergeant said. 'You should have asked for his papers.'

'He's been in that state ever since,' the old woman explained.

'How long?'

'Two days.'

'Search the house,' the sergeant ordered.

The soldiers flung themselves on the fishing equipment and all the rest of the hut's contents, upsetting everything.

'They were lying,' said a very unmasculine voice.

'We were not lying,' the old woman retorted.

'What's this, then?'

The soldier held up Dadou's bag, from which he had just extracted letters, photographs, papers, and a sheaf of banknotes. He handed the photos, money, and papers to the sergeant.

'Nationality Angolan,' the sergeant read.

With a cruel smile of triumph he turned Dadou over with his foot until he was lying on his back. Then he stepped on his stomach to see if he was shamming.

'They have tough hides, these Resistance people,' he stated, kicking Dadou repeatedly in the ribs. 'Sleep like logs while I'm being eaten alive by mosquitoes.'

He began to pant with rage and exertion. His feet must have been hurting, too, he was kicking so violently — the way a man might lay his axe to an extra-hard tree trunk. He was waiting for the cry, one cry at least.

'Take them all away,' he yelled, rolling up his sleeves. 'We'll deal with this somewhere else. I'll get a peep out of him — see if I don't.'

13

Yealdara reached the fishing village early one morning.

For the sake of prudence and because things were still sticky politically, she had asked the governor to supply her with Congolese papers. The governor had lost a lot of his contacts over the Dadou affair. And since the traffic in papers was 'big business', hence only for high-ups, nearly four months had passed before the governor found a 'taker', whereas Dadou's papers had taken him only three days.

'Don't write to me,' the governor had insisted. 'Whatever happens. I'm convinced they know my code name. They think I'm an enemy agent. They're having me watched. Dadou was a man. With all a man's beauty and all a man's nobility. I helped him. There was no resisting that face. But sometimes the greatest thing you can do in the world is something for your own skin. And you do it. Oh, yes. Because you want to get the better of yourself. The trouble starts when you come to take stock, try to add things up — and find a deficit. When it begins to look like suicide. And you say to yourself: what's the point of dying for someone like Dadou? What good will it have done, dying for a hundred, ten thousand, a million Dadous? You can tell him that from me. If at least he had amounted to something, like Christ or Mao, I'd be proud of what I did for him. Justice. Yes, possibly. But what good is an ounce of justice in an ocean of shit? Tell him to fight if he can. Because it's driving me mad, knowing a swine like that has wrecked my whole life and he can't even use his fists.'

The governor had done a lot of grumbling that evening. Then he had slipped the sheaf of Congolese papers into Yealdara's hands with a smile.

'I'm like your dog,' he said. 'If he's human, let him fight. So that my deeds shan't be silences. Let him find something to bloody do with a life like his, for God's sake!'

At the fishing village Dadou's traces had disappeared. And Yealdara tried to see in the sand. The first villager to whom she had dared to mention old Fortuné, otherwise known as Sacramento, had the kindness to explain to her that that was a dangerous name.

'It's a Resistance fighter's name, ma'am. And here you've only got to mention a Resistance fighter's name more than once and you land in jail.'

'He's not a Resistance fighter. Fortuné isn't that sort.'

'They took him for one. Here people are what they're taken for.'

The old fisherman lowered his voice: 'If I wasn't an old friend of Fortuné's I'd have gone and told them you were mentioning names of Resistance fighters. And they'd come and get you. You see, miss. . .'

The old man was not sure whether he gave this ravishing stranger greater pleasure by addressing her as an unmarried or as a married woman.

'You see, ma'am. . . A stranger came here talking about

Fortuné two or three months ago. Well, they found him down by the river, beaten half to death. And a few days later the soldiers arrived. They even picked up the people who had given the stranger shelter. We haven't seen them since. That means they've kept them, which suggests they smelled a rat. My name's Amando. Twenty-seven years I've been here. I came here because it's as if all the ordinary people, all the people who have suffered, all the people who have lost out in life, have to come here. I can see it in your eyes. I reckon you too, ma'am. . . What's your name?'

'Yealdara.'

'So it's miss?'

'Yes.'

'Ah, forgive me. I am utterly stupid. It's obvious from your face that you are not a married woman.'

'What was he like, the stranger who talked about Fortuné'

'I was on the river when they came. We lamprey fishermen, you know, spend whole seasons on the river. I was told he had long hair and a heavy beard. A good-looking fellow in his early thirties.'

'Where did they take him?'

'Where do they take Resistance fighters?'

'The stranger wasn't a Resistance fighter.'

'He certainly looked like one!'

Prudently, Yealdara did not repeat her question about where they took Resistance fighters. She gave herself two days to think things over. Two days of hell. On the third day, her decision taken, she went back to see Amando.

'Is there something you want?'

'Yes. A favour. You know, don't you, that one must help people who have "lost out in life". Spread a rumour that I'm a Resistance fighter.'

'What's this all about?'

'You'll be doing me a favour.'

'No, I refuse.'

'Why?'

'But ma'am — don't you realize they kill Resistance fighters?'

In his emotion old Amando had forgotten to address Yealdara as 'miss'. He looked at her as at one returned from the dead.

'What's this all about?' he asked again.

'Do me this favour,' Yealdara insisted.

'No. I shan't. Even if you were a Resistance fighter. A fisherman of my standing, a fisherman of my age sells fish, not human beings.'

'I want to find out. . .'

'Ma'am,' said the old man, 'believe me when I tell you they kill Resistance fighters. That's what they expect, isn't it?'

Yealdara went back to the old hut on the river bank where the people had put her up on her arrival. It had belonged to an old madwoman, who one day decided to find out what there was at the bottom of the river. Her name had been Lanza. The villagers used to say she had gone mad from having eaten her husband. On her death another madwoman from the village had moved into the hut. It was where all suspect strangers were lodged. Beside the hut stood the tree they called the 'owl tree', a tall mango in which owls came and sat each night as if in conference.

The sun at that time of the evening was lovely on the river. Yealdara questioned at length the waters sliding by. She thought about the catfish nation, the carp race, the crab tribe, the leech families, the house of the burbot. She thought about peace, about happiness, and about love. For the fish, there was man. It was less sordid, though. She thought about so many things that she fell asleep.

She woke to find the old man squatting on the ground. Yealdara folded her mat. She was very hungry. For a long time she was silent, unable to think of anything to say to the old man. Amando was silent too, not daring to speak. They looked at each other like that, in silence, for nearly ten minutes.

'I am sure in my mind that all those who suffer, all those who've lost out in life have to come here.'

'Why?' came Yealdara's voice.

'No reason,' said the old man. 'Just to come.'

'How have you suffered?'

'They killed my wife and my three sons during the war of liberation. After Independence they decided I was a traitor. I was wanted dead or alive. I cleared off. I'm breathing, but inside me life is over. And the flesh, and the blood — both over. I'm breathing. I've a feeling you are in much the same case.'

'No,' Yealdara said.

'Your eyes tell me you have suffered.'

Yealdara told old Amando all about Dadou. The whole story.

'He's not a member of the Resistance. He came here to find peace.'

'It's the Resistance fighters' fault,' said the old man. 'They come through here and everybody is taken for one of them.'

'Do you think they will have killed him?'

Yealdara contemplated the peaceful river gliding past.

'Men are unworthy of this world,' she said.

The old man nodded approvingly.

'What do you plan to do, ma'am?'

This time Amando had really not wanted to call her 'miss'. In fact he had decided to call her nothing but 'ma'am' in future.

Yealdara gave him a long look. 'There is no reason why they should kill him. And if God has a chance to do his bit, he will live. He has a right to life.'

'Yes — come the Resurrection,' Amando said.

'Man has no need of the Resurrection as long as life is his due.'

'There's no knowing when life is entirely our due. We cannot say it's at the moment when we are losing it. My advice to you is: stay here and wait. Maybe heaven will send something.'

'Do you believe that?'

'Oh, we still believe here. In this place, you see, belief becomes a duty. Belief in all those who have fallen. On behalf of all those who will fall. Believe or die — that's the only choice left to us. One day this world will be over. Like that of the Luanda Portuguese.'

'That's poor consolation,' Yealdara said. 'What I believe is that every generation has the right to live its life. Every man has the right to the shape and sound of his breathing. The rest is all snares. Snares that some people set to catch others.'

They talked until nightfall. Yealdara had drawn up a kind of scale of things: 'It is more sordid to be killed by a man than by starvation. It is less sordid to be killed by a Belgian than by a black.' Amando, to upset the scale, went further:

'The joy, the great joy of it is that we are at the beginning of the end. Each one of us that falls is a solid step nearer the end. And all of us here have only one wish: the end. We should be miserable were it not for the end. Have you eaten?'

'No,' said Yealdara. 'I'm hungry.'

'Let's go to my place. I have some fish. There's no manioc anywhere. But I have some yams. We'll eat Angolan-style.'

She stood up. Amando was looking at her with the eyes of a father. She understood. She collected her bits and pieces and wrapped them in her mat. When she had tied the bundle the old man took it and carried it for her.

'I'll arrange to get you some local papers.'

'I have local papers,' Yealdara said.

'One less worry!' the old man exclaimed. 'This is a mad world. It's only papers that argue now, only papers that think, only papers that breathe. Men, all men, have got stuck — hearts, heads, bloodstreams. Papers are the only blood still circulating.'

Yealdara laid out her mat and slept like a log. The old man lit his pipe and smoked. He stayed awake all night. He watched over Yealdara, and from time to time he knelt to pray to God.

But he could not think what to pray for. In this country a girl so pretty ought not to have so ugly a life. Surely there was something that could be done for her. City folk used plenty of sex. Amando, however, had no intention of doing anything dirty with her. He was thinking more in terms of finding her (or letting time come up with) a well-brought-up suitor who would install her in a life at the top. Or, if she really was God's, she would spend her days fishing in peace and tranquillity. The river was still the home of the great souls of these parts. This last idea put him in mind of an old custom where he came from: when a man was good and dead they used him to catch fish; they tied his body in a wicker fish-trap, they found a place where there were plenty of fish, and they caught the fish using the body as bait. The custom had died out, but it had left traces in people's memories.

14

Yealdara went fishing with Amando. It was all there was for her to do.

Time passed: weeks, months. Towards the end of the year Amando started sending her into the town to sell the fish they had caught and to purchase equipment. The river wore everything out, gobbled everything up. She is young and beautiful, he thought, she will never have any trouble over papers. The old man began to hope that Yealdara would quickly find a suitor with a splendid position in society. All the beautiful girls in the country knew their way around in this respect and invariably found a solid taker. When they were not satisfied they went on looking, and they always ended up finding what they wanted. The local men were great consumers of women, and the prices were quite respectable. It was even believed that often when they fought it was to get into the positions that would allow them to consume the 'choicest morsels'.

The old man went on hoping for Yealdara. But if Yealdara lingered in town, coming out of one shop to go into another, strolling down one street after another, it was in case, among all the faces, she should meet a pair of eyes that belonged to Dadou. She had found out about the kinds of drink consumed in the town and the places where they were sold. She had found out about the shots available, Dadou having succumbed to shots back on the other side of the river. She stayed longer than the old man had said to stay. But when she got back he always understood. And she took advantage of the old man's great kindness to stay even longer next time and to make her visits more frequent. She had the occasional mishap, yet she always managed to escape without, as the expression had it, 'getting her legs dirty'. The old man gave her enough money for her clothes and for a bit of finery. In this town a bit of finery was a universally accepted ticket of admission at every level of society. Yealdara was aware of the old man's hopes for her. She was loath to smash those hopes by opening her heart to him.

Here, to be duped was often the surest and greatest form of happiness. So much so that some people actually worked at it. Others simply abandoned themselves to drink or drugs. *Absolute power absolutely guarantees social imbalance.* 'Who said that?' Yealdara wondered. Not Dadou. The old man, probably. And now, idling about the streets of the city, all she could think of was that sentence. She had others in her head, maybe right, maybe wrong. One thing she was sure of: all these countries were heading for the dark. People will kill one another, people will cry out, and that will be all they can do. She recalled the night they had sat up talking until three o'clock. And the old man had said: 'Heaven, that's probably a long way off, a very long way off. But hell — at least if we keep walking we'll get to hell.'

Three days in the town. She could have stayed another one or two. But her heart told her to return to the village. She listened to her heart a lot. A young man driving a Mercedes offered her a lift as far as the Galbara Bridge. She accepted. The town slid past beneath the wheels. All was quiet. No one asked to see their papers, not even at the bridge. The young man wanted to drive her all the way to the village.

'No,' Yealdara said. 'It's too sandy. Cars can't get that far.'

'But a Mercedes. . .'

'It wouldn't get there.'

'We could try.'

'You can't make a road fit for a Mercedes out of sand and mud.'

The young man was very upset. But maybe she was right. The thought of having to push the Mercedes with a girl. . .

'What's your name? Mine's Marti. Can I give you my card?'

'If you like.'

'Here. It might get you out of an awkward situation some time.'

When the young man had gone Yealdara read the card: 'Marti Mouyabas, attaché to the Presidency of the Republic. Commander of the Special Forces, P.O. Box 4021, tel.: 84-12-81.'

She walked for a long time before she reached the taxi-bus stop. Taxi-buses covered the stretch to within eight kilometres of the fishing village. The taxi-bus took a while to arrive. She waited two hours.

Back at the village Yealdara was surprised to find the governor in the old man's hut. She shook hands without speaking. What was happening over there? It was the fashion now. People from over there were coming here. People from here were going over there. Fleeing from one bank to land on the other. But which was the more to be fled from? It was hard to say. One just went ahead. Life was much the same on both banks. The frontier was for papers. Papers, however, had been overcome.

'He says he's a friend,' the old man announced.

'He's a friend,' said Yealdara.

'He came across yesterday.'

'Are things going wrong over there?'

'No. Your father had me fired. But they didn't stop there. They accused me of having made an attempt on the life of the Commissar-General of the People.'

'What's the Commissar-General of the People?'

'Don't you listen to the radio?'

'I threw my set in the river.'

'A district president is now called a Commissar-General of the People. A bomb went off. And I got the blame. For the simple reason that I could prove it was your father who'd done it.'

'If I'm ever able to go back there,' Yealdara said, 'it will be to kill my father.'

'You won't leave here,' said the old man. 'Here we are outside the world, but we're happy. We have the river. We have the land. Let's leave them their world. Here we have quite enough to wait for the end.'

'The end,' echoed Yealdara with a sigh. 'Well, I don't need the end.'

'You'll have no peace,' said the old man.

'I don't need peace.'

'What is it you're looking for?'

'A haven.'

'A haven.' It was the old man's turn to sigh. 'The only haven is the end for those who are not duped.'

The governor entered quickly into the life of the village. Soon he could fish as well as Yealdara and Amando. Sometimes they laughed at the fresh smell of the fish awaiting death in the bottom of the canoe. They laughed at the wildly racing river. Sadness came in the evenings, when they revived their memories of Dadou, when that name beat in their chests like a second heart, when it shone out of their eyes. Sadness came when Yealdara sang the 'hits' of the musicians from across the river and her great eyes became swollen with who knew what invincible demons, who knew what fierce hope. And when she began to challenge God.

'If only you could do your bit! If only you could show yourself and understand that he had a right to happiness!'

'Stop blaspheming,' the governor scolded. 'Don't talk about things you don't understand.'

'Something keeps whispering to me that he's alive. I wish I knew what.'

The question of the governor's papers began to arise. The old man had tried but had lost track of the man who used to supply him with papers in exchange for a basket of fish. People in the town were always starving. So they were always ready to help you. It was just a matter of finding a decent sort. You could easily get yourself swindled. The people who had taken your all turned round and said: 'Things are getting difficult. Let's wait till they settle down a bit.' You waited months, years. They knew you would never go lodging a complaint. So everything went along quite amicably. Everything went along the way it always does in that sort of business.

'We have to find you some local papers,' the old man said. 'But it's getting to be a problem. On account of the latest disturbances.'

'I have an address,' said Yealdara.

She rummaged among her things and came up with the card Marti had given her. The old man took it, read it. He shook his head.

'This fellow's too big for this kind of thing. We'll need him another time, for other problems. Papers are more petty-clerk level. I'll try again. I'll find someone.'

But the soldiers called at the fishing village. The governor was taken away. For Yealdara and Amando it was hard. The blows. The falls. The insults. The levelled guns. Why did God not do his bit? The rifle was becoming a heart. But a hard heart.

There was fighting. And people fell. Here, there, everywhere. The trigger had become a brain. The gun a soul. And there was firing. And people fell. What could you call it but a dog's life in a dog's world?

'Oh, what are you waiting for, Lord,' the old man breathed, 'before you start taking a hand? The killing! The killing! What a time! What a country! What men! Not that men even count any more, not really. Or if they do it's simply because their heads can roll. And heads are rolling — here, there, and everywhere.'

Yealdara was weeping. The old man attempted to console her. But each word he uttered turned into a stone that came back and hit him in the eyes. He tried his best, but eventually he was weeping himself.

'This isn't right,' he said, wiping away Yealdara's tears and letting his own flow down his cheeks.

Mucus filled his nostrils as he tried to repeat: 'It's human to weep for the living.'

'You think they're alive?'

'I don't know,' said the old man. 'But we've no real reason to think they're dead.'

'They're dead,' Yealdara said.

'They're alive,' said the old man.

'I'd need to see them first.'

'We can think it.'

'Well, I think they're dead.'

'And I think they're alive. The truly dead are the ones where you've seen the body — like my wife, like my children, my three boys. The rest are alive — or they're "maybe-alives". With "maybe-alives" you can ask God for them to be truly alive. That's the beginning. . .'

'Don't talk any more — it hurts,' Yealdara said.

'It hurts me too,' the old man said, 'but I have to. I was telling you the other day that all who have suffered have to come here. I believed that. But when people start to leave even this place, that's the last straw. What we need is the end, not the last straw.'

They had got into the habit of talking every evening after their fish soup. Their daily bread they had. They would go on having it as long as they stayed where they were. But peace, no. Happiness is not bread; it is what is behind the bread. Happiness is peace of mind, peace of soul, peace of the blood, the eyes, the ears, the arse. But as long as people went on leaving — leaving places there is no getting away from! — there would be everything except what matters. There would be everything except love and peace. There would be poverty. Physical and moral. There would be no men. Only animals lying in wait for one another, hunting one another down, killing one another for reasons more vile and sordid than those of a leopard tearing the life from a doe. There would be physical and moral wounds such as Yealdara's and the old man's. There would be flies. There would be reason to spit.

'This is the land where things are more tender than anywhere in the world. The sky, the river, the vegetation — everything is tender. Yet it is over this divine tenderness of everything that men kill one another. How absurd to think of them immolating themselves over this feast of living things.'

'It certainly is,' the old man echoed. 'So absurd that it leads us into our own absurdities. We begin to think that the men in the jungle are right, that they're fighting for a just "cause". But when they take over the town, when they take over the girls and the drink supplies and the cars, who is to say they won't act exactly like the town people today? Who's to say they won't likewise start killing peaceable innocents? (Even if this is the land of the guilty — a land where no one is entirely innocent any more.)'

'Let's not talk about it. Let's talk about fish and the river. Otherwise we'll go mad. Let's talk about the sand and the canoes. That's what is left to us of this world. That and the end.'

'That and the end,' the old man repeated after her. 'In ten or twenty years' time, you know, our children will hate soldiers the way we hated the colonists. And the new decolonization will begin. The most important revolution, the first one: the soldier exchanged for the heart and the intellect. If that can happen there will be no end any more. There will be the beginning. I prefer the beginning. Hatred will be a thing of the past. Blood, bodies, the soldiers. Then we shall have our Marxes and Lenins and Maos, our Christs and Mahomets and Shakespeares, our soulmates.'

The old man spoke as if reading what he was saying somewhere on the walls of the hut. His eyes were hard and his face strong. His white hair seemed to stand up and mark time with his words. He spoke so much he went into a trance. Outside the hut the night was fine, with the majestic shadow of the river and the sky studded a million times with stars staring down like eyes. It would be a great consolation to die anywhere, anyhow, and of anything on such a night.

'. . . Here we are seeing the birth of a phenomenon that is becoming progressively natural and that is called "putridity". And that is why we live and die in this most putrid of all worlds. It used to be good here, with the river, the fish, men. And as I used to say up until a very short while ago: this was still a place where those could come who had "lost" — I used to say lost but I must correct myself because those who die here are the "winners of the world", the winners of things, of everything. They're the winners of the "way".'

Yealdara was already asleep on her half-unrolled mat. But the old man went ranting on.

'. . . This is the most sordid time there has ever been, they're saying so everywhere. And the most sordid time there has ever been listens and laughs its head off. He'll come, he will eventually. Today we're preparing the way for him, we're fishing for him, we're doing his publicity work. And when he comes, I'm telling you, when he comes. . .'

The old man noticed that Yealdara was fast asleep. He spread his own mat and lay for a long time smoking his pipe. He put out the oil lamp and the darkness closed in around his pipe, a little smiling eye of fire.

There were other calm nights when the old man talked for as long as he had that night, when he went into a trance, when Yealdara eventually gave in to her eyelids despite the force of the old man's utterances, when she fell asleep on the bare ground without the old man noticing, when he spread the mat beneath her already stiffened limbs. Time came and went, bearing away its burden of events that devoured so many friends, so many acquaintances, so much hope, so much strength. Leaving the river between its two banks. Leaving the sky. And leaving a mat for the old man, for Yealdara, and for so many others in so many fishing villages.

15

Five years had flowed by like water. The river still had fish in it. Amando and Yealdara went fishing. And when the baskets were good and full he sent her into town to sell the contents. For two or three weeks she stayed with an old woman Amando knew.

They had sold a lot of fish that season. Because of the shortage of food throughout the country and especially in the town the price of fish had risen at a rate that was bad for the buyer but providential for the seller. Yealdara sold to bulk buyers and was regarded as a kind of wholesaler, even though the amounts she sold were modest. There were the little presents to sweeten the clients and keep them sweet. Bloody town! It was a question of spending as little time there as possible. And if you wanted to do that you had to sell your stuff quickly. The mother of all quick-selling techniques was the smile. The smile and the tip.

This time she had been in town for ten days. The fish had been difficult to sell because things were 'sticky'. Thanks to her smile, however, Yealdara had been successful. All the way back she had shown her smile and her papers. Her smile first, then her papers. She was no longer young, but her body had retained all the magical qualities of her sex, as Amando used to say. That was why Yealdara had been able to go around with five-year-old papers in defiance of all advice and despite the changes of colour and size that the national identity card — the most important of them — had undergone in the meantime. She had been able to get by without a green 'devotion-to-the-cause' card.

Back at the village, a neighbour came to tell her that they had taken the old man away.

'I'll sell myself for him,' she said, her voice expressionless. 'I'll give myself.'

She thought of the visiting-card handed to her by the attaché to the Presidency, whose name she could not even remember. She searched every inch of the hut: the card was nowhere to be found in the mess the soldiers had left. That damned address. Yealdara was sure it was hidden there somewhere. She continued to search far into the night, knowing that she was hardly likely to sleep anyway.

'That little cretin in the Mercedes has put a spell on his bloody card,' she thought. 'He must have been here and put a spell on it.'

She went on looking. She was still looking when the first cock crowed. Then the idea of giving up became lodged in her brain. So much had happened in five years that an attaché to the Presidency was almost certain to have been shaken loose by now. In fact his name might be mud or worse. His name might be a prison door — if not a ticket to a violent death. Yealdara wondered what was the best course. She could not decide. With her out-of-date papers it was wiser for her to avoid the town. She had already considered 'the bottom of the river'. But such a death was as dark and gloomy as life. Frightened by the idea, she had resolved to drive it out vigorously whenever it entered her head.

'Life is now so bloody awful here — every kind of life has become so putrid here that the most brilliant career a man can have is not worth that of a stupid fly.'

She determined to go on the river early. The water slid by beneath the canoe. She tried to dream but grim reality assailed and cruelly tormented her.

'I've got to fight. My hands are not tied yet. My body isn't done for yet. As long as there's a drop of blood left in me, I shall fight. And my first efforts must be directed at finding that address. Dadou, the governor, the old man, Sacramento, Henri, Sylvain, the old woman — they're all "maybe-alives". If they are alive, they're fighting, and if they're fighting, then I must fight too. In this place reality — the only reality — is breathing in order to fight. And going on breathing until they overcome you.'

That evening, paddling back, she had two fat fish in the bottom of the canoe. She wanted to dream, at least to dream. The river and its colours in the setting sun made dreaming possible. The sky, stained with gold, silver, copper, and purple, was overwhelming in its purity. 'No,' she thought, 'this is no place to die a putrid death. Everything is a lesson to the heart, a lesson in life. Everything is swelling, expanding. Seek, it all says. But to seek is to find, and if you find you're finished.' She thought of the bottom of the river. The crabs. The fish. The stones. It was dark at the bottom of the river. As dark as the depths of her love for Dadou, as dark as the depths of what she felt for the old man and the others. Dark but not dejected. You can't deject something like the bottom of the river.

She moored her canoe. Weariness. She picked up the fish and set out for the village. Night was falling. The stars were starting to reassemble in the sky. Pure nature, Yealdara thought, holy nature. Get rid of all the men and everything becomes God. As

she walked she pushed aside the tall grass that blocked the
path. The glow-worms were lighting up, swinging their dead
fires. A thousand insects opened up with their calls and whistles
and songs. How, with this feast going on, have men chosen to be
miserable?

'They will kill them all, like so many fish, if they haven't
killed them already. They'll kill us all like rats. And God will do
nothing. And nothing will do nothing. One hope is left to us,
and only one "May death be a way", in the words of the
ancestors.'

The hut struck her as empty, vast, bitter. She thought for a
long time about the old man. She thought about Dadou and the
others. The old man had had the word for it: 'maybe-alives.'
Yes, but she wanted them there. To talk to. To listen to. To
discuss things, laugh together, make plans. Tonight. While this
desire for life was on her. To speak their names. Echo their
gestures. But suppose they are dead, she thought. No. Always
corpses, corpses to overflowing. Gaining ground at every level,
filling all the key jobs. The corpse is a loathsome formality. The
crushing invasion. The mounting tide. The blockage. Above all
if they died an ugly death, a putrid death. If they were told to
run and then shot in the back. If they fell face up, eyes still open,
staring at the sky. And if the flies came. If they had their hands
together at their chests like priests at prayer.

She resumed her search for the attaché's address. The young
man had looked quite naive, with a naive smile. She would be
able to extract favours from him without 'getting her legs dirty'.
Or, if matters refused to shift at that level of operation, she
would let him. . . Afterwards she would scrub herself with all
the soap in the world. And it would go. Conscience. Well,
conscience just had to face up to reality.

At last she found the address. 'God be praised!' she breathed
with a sigh. 'I thought the mice had eaten it. I'll go there
tomorrow.'

She read aloud: 'Marti Mouyabas. . .'

She recovered her smile. She was counting on him now, first of all for papers because papers were becoming a priority. After that, she would decide whether to have a word with him about the old man and the others. She laid out her mat and went to sleep with the visiting-card of Marti Mouyabas tucked in her top.

Next morning Yealdara got up before dawn. She set out for the town immediately after her bath. This time she waited a good twenty minutes for the taxi-bus.

The town was swarming with soldiers. She was asked for her papers every hundred yards. She showed them with the visiting-card on top. It worked so well that she decided to show only the visiting-card. This worked much better than with the papers. And instead of her usual smile she adopted a dignified look. To such effect that often, as they handed back the card, the soldiers added a respectful 'Our apologies, ma'am', which almost went to her head. Now it was their turn to quake with fear. To roast her victims Yealdara always added a motherly smile.

She went straight to the house of the kindest of the old man's acquaintances, the one she stayed with when selling fish in the town. This was an elderly woman called Bambara. She cried for a long time on hearing that the old man had been arrested. Yealdara attempted to console her but without success.

'They may kill him.'

'He's innocent.'

'It's the innocent ones they kill.'

'God will help him. Surely God will manage to do something for him.'

'Things here have got beyond God. This is a heavy world. A heavy time.'

She wept the whole afternoon and all through the night. How she must have loved the old man!

Yealdara bought paper and an envelope. Contriving a few
sweet words for Marti, she invited him to meet her in the park
on Sunday morning. She said she would wait for him until nine
o'clock. She posted the letter and went shopping for things to
give a man a thrill. She had the physical endowments to bowl a
man over.

Dadou! Perhaps Dadou was a man and a half, as people over
there said. And anyway, she had not failed utterly. He did not
love her. He had even preferred Yavelde. But had he not
eventually told her (and it was his word) that she had a
sensational body? Everything about her gave her confidence,
even her age. Even the strange state of nerves that constricted
her chest and clouded her gaze. Today was Thursday. Time
would fly. And if that little cretin with the Mercedes had got her
letter he would come. Men, especially in the upper reaches of
society, set great store by this particular item.

Sunday morning arrived. Yealdara's get-up offended old
Bambara.

'You're a callous one, living it up when your friends are
dead.'

Yealdara said nothing. She went out into the street. It was
raining. She slipped a small boy a franc to go as far as the
made-up road and fetch her a taxi. He did very well: he came
back with a 404, one of the smart ones.

'Take me to the park.'

'Sorry,' said the driver. 'We can't go there today.'

'Whyever not?'

'There's a guard on it.'

'A guard?'

'Distinguished visitors staying in the street adjoining.'

Rage boiled over in Yealdara's brain and doused her body
with bitter lassitude. She was powerless. The park was called
Freedom Park: why did they speak of freedom in a world where
everything was barred? It is when men stoop so low that a
person really needs God. Yealdara decided to go to church.

With the Protestants of Omega or the Catholics of Montagne-des-Douze. Or the Moslems of the Étoile district, for that matter. She walked a very long way. She needed that walk through the mud and the pools of stagnant water. She needed to smell the town, which so resembled other towns: it helped to blot out the smell of her sociology diplomas, which something or other had revived.

At the church of St Nicholas, Yealdara was astonished by the number of tearful faces calling on God.

'He really must come. He has to come eventually.'

Things were getting too bad. All roads were blocked. The only one left open was hope. All rights were dead but the right to hope — to illusions, perhaps. And there was one mighty word that jostled every heart and mind and body. That word was 'perhaps'. She tried to think of the angels organized in a celestial army. About to put the world to rout with one flourish on their trumpets.

'If God does not come, there will never be peace here. People are killing one another, hunting one another down, setting traps for one another, lying in wait. . .'

She sang along with the other worshippers, her mind on that little cretin of an attaché.

'They might have waited for another day to close the park. If there's a real clamp-down I'll be in serious trouble with these papers. He could help me. I should have put my address. I'm a fool, a wretched fool.'

You came to church to get away from the outside world. But the outside world hunted you down everywhere. It surrounded you. It tightened on you like a terrible knot, it bit into you, scratched at you, pricked you, beset you. The outside world was the new wild animal of these parts that leapt on you at the slightest opportunity and tore at your flesh, crunched your bones. It moved like a tidal wave and behaved like an earthquake running right through all being, beneath all flesh and blood, deep within every consciousness.

Yealdara had been following the mass with half an ear. They had asked God to help the country and its rulers. They had asked God to give it love and peace. What hypocrisy — asking God to do the job of men, as if men had ever tried to do God's.

Afterwards she walked at random through the streets of the town, studying all the cars. That Marti was damned special if he did not drive his Mercedes down Fanfare Street. Several streets later she felt a terrible urge to ask the first passer-by if he knew Marti Mouyabas. The country was so small and the people who made up its high society so few that everyone knew them all. Then, if chance so willed. . . But her nerve failed her. With her awful papers, if she happened on a. . . She did not dare. She went on walking.

She came upon a madman. He was striding along in front of her with a mat beneath his left arm and a stick in his right hand. Yealdara quickened her pace and caught up with him. As she passed him the madman promptly turned on his heel. She had taken another five or six paces before she too turned and retraced her steps. At the corner of the street the madman began running as fast as his legs would carry him.

'Dadou!' Yealdara cried.

But the madman went on running. She dared not try to run herself (her long dress, her papers). Yealdara was sure the madman was Dadou. She worked it out for herself: 'He must have escaped. And in order to avoid being asked for his papers he has chosen to pass for insane. He's not in the least insane really.'

She stayed in that district for a while but without finding any trace of the madman. She covered every street, her eyes examining every little turning. She considered mirages. Out she had seen Dadou plainly. It could not have been anyone else. She would take a census of all the madmen in the town. Why had he run away, though? He had recognized her. Yealdara was sure he had recognized her.

She had begun her madman hunt next morning, when she encountered some thirty of them at liberty. She had been hunting for nearly a fortnight now, combing the central districts first, then the outlying districts. She decided to visit the asylum.

One morning Yealdara, still in her finery, had left Bambara's house and was walking along thinking about Henri, Sylvain, the old man, Sacramento, and the others. Her eyes were slightly swollen with the tears that slept in them. She had been asked for her papers five or six times and had presented them with the attaché's visiting-card and a dignified smile. The method was too successful for her not to have continued to make use of it.

'Every madman in this town. Every madman in the world, if need be. I must call them all to account. One of them has to be him.'

She was walking along, engrossed in her monologue, when she was stopped once again.

'May I see your papers, ma'am?'

'Here you are.'

She presented the visiting-card first, then the old national identity card, then the 'devotion-to-the-cause' card, then the Party and Women's Assembly cards. It was always in that strategic order that Yealdara presented her papers.

'Why have you not had this identity card changed yet, ma'am?'

'Those offices work slowly, brother.'

'Not for important ladies like yourself,' the sergeant smiled.

'I wonder if you could help me.'

'A fellow doesn't help the society ladies. It can land him in trouble.'

'Do you know Marti Mouyabas personally?'

'A fellow can't call himself a militant if he doesn't know the First Secretary personally.'

'Could you do me a small favour on his behalf?'

For a long time the sergeant hesitated. Women belonging to bigshots were women who spelled trouble. Everyone knew that. His eyebrows crinkled, then straightened.

'What do you want me to do?' he asked, all smiles.

'You command a unit. Do you have transport?'

'The car is for the people's business only.'

'I'll introduce you to Marti in person.'

'I can't drive. I have myself driven.'

'Have me driven,' Yealdara said.

The sergeant called over to a man who was dozing on his rifle in the shade of a mango tree: 'Corporal! Do you know the First Secretary's place?'

'Mouyabas?'

'Yes.'

'Office or home?'

The sergeant repeated the question to Yealdara.

'His home,' said Yealdara.

'Take the lady there.'

Yealdara introduced herself to Mrs Mouyabas as a young militant who wished to see the First Secretary on official business. Mrs Mouyabas showed her into the reception room. Yealdara remembered her own house on the other side of the river. She thought of her mat back in the fishing village.

Life is a scandal. All life. All lives. This country where people were dying in chains — why did God not take a hand? Why did he not open a way to men? This world was blocked, stopped-up, done for. It needed someone a lot cleverer than men to get it out of this one. This hole. The huge hole of madness that was forming here; the plagues, the downpour.

Marti Mouyabas emerged from his office. Quickly Yealdara thought what she must say to the First Secretary in front of his wife. She exuded politeness, respect, apologies.

'I missed you at your office, Comrade First Secretary.'

Marti Mouyabas said nothing at first, evidently searching among the myriad women who bore his life along for the moment when he might have met this face. A face worthy of him. When Mrs Mouyabas finally made up her mind to leave them alone, not without deciding to pop back from time to time on some excuse to pick up bits of their conversation, Yealdara handed Mouyabas the visiting-card.

'Five years ago,' he breathed. 'But I don't understand.'

'You didn't get my letter, then. . .'

Mrs Mouyabas came in with glasses.

'A large champagne for me,' the First Secretary broke in. 'And will madam comrade drink something?'

'Fruit juice,' said Yealdara.

'Ah, no!' protested Marti Mouyabas, taking advantage of this diversion to drop the subject of the letter. 'You're not going to disgrace your station, madam comrade. Anyway, no one drinks the sweat of the orange tree in this house. Bring her a Saint-Clément, darling,' he told his wife, to get rid of her.

'Strange names they have for their wines,' Yealdara thought. Strange names they have for everything.'

'If the problem that brings you here. . . But, darling, it ought to have ice in it.'

Mrs Mouyabas went off to find ice — a job that left them three minutes. Yealdara put her papers problem in a few concise words; the First Secretary gave her his latest visiting-card together with his personal telephone number. The ice cubes had delayed her drink but that was fine: they had kept Mrs Mouyabas in the kitchen. The rest of the interview consisted mainly of conspiratorial glances and smiles. Yealdara made her mark on the First Secretary through her warmth and through her smell. Her great beauty stirred Mouyabas deeply. He hoped — since his wife looked like staying in the room now — that she would telephone. He swallowed a mouthful of saliva as he watched her leave, the play of her haunches like a saxophone solo.

'Oh, the lust,' he thought. 'And just look at those lines!'

16

At the price of three weekends spent with Mouyabas at his so-called 'Villa de Corteza', Yealdara now had papers sound enough to stand any amount of inspection. But she dared not talk about Dadou or about the old man or any of the others.

'My tender goddess,' Mouyabas would say.

And Yealdara would switch off her body to stop herself crying out. She would stop up her heart and her whole being. She had grown accustomed to being stripped like a piece of meat by a man who stank of drink, tobacco, and sham. One day she thought of killing him.

She had stayed in bed. Mouyabas had finished.

'My tender goddess! I shall spend every weekend with you here. You shall be my favourite. You'll always be my favourite.'

Now he was taking a bath. Yealdara read the visiting-card again: Martin Nzoma Mouyabas, alias Prosondo, First Secretary with responsibility for Co-ordination, Press, and

Propaganda — Permanent Member, P.O. Box 4023, tel.: 21-25-18. . .

Time, Yealdara thought. What was she to do with all the wretched time falling like rain inside her? She looked at her body. She wanted to spit. She spat on Mouyabas's sheets. For all the girls who had been there before her. For all the ones who were waiting and would come there in future. She bit her underlip in such irritation that she hurt herself.

Mouyabas was getting dressed. He came over and planted a kiss on her thighs. 'He's a charming brute,' Yealdara thought. He had undoubtedly betrayed and killed people to have got where he was. Having got there, the first thing he did was to start 'laying women'. But that was the price of papers here. And you had to have papers, or die like a fly. 'Disappear', they called it. Yealdara bit her underlip again. Mouyabas brought her a cup of coffee.

'Thank you,' she said.

'Are you coming back to town?'

'Yes.'

'You come back by taxi. I don't want anyone going to her with stories and that starting fights at home. She has lookouts posted everywhere. And it's my money the bitch pays them with. Don't spoil your groundwork.'

'I'll be careful,' Yealdara said. 'Groundwork is everything nowadays. When you've done it well, you look after it.'

'You know, you stagger me. You're the kind of woman who drives men crazy. Has anyone ever told you that?'

'No,' said Yealdara.

Mouyabas sat on the bed and leant his head back on Yealdara's legs. He began to breathe deeply, making his lips quiver. His eyes were closed.

'The lion,' Yealdara thought. 'Behold the lion in the lap of sex.'

She plugged his nostrils by inserting her second and third fingers. Mouyabas held on heroically to show her how much puff he had. When she did not remove her fingers from his nostrils he started breathing through his mouth. She poured some coffee into it. Mouyabas spluttered explosively.

'You. . . you. . .'

'Don't talk.'

Mouyabas went on coughing for a long time before he calmed down.

He began kissing her all over.

'You've never. . . You don't. . .'

Yealdara laid a trembling hand over his mouth.

'I want us to get to know each other now,' Mouyabas said.

'I never talk about myself,' said Yealdara.

'Why not?'

'This body had a right to love, to peace, to happiness, to life. I believed in it the way one believes in God. Then I lost it, it eluded me. Everything eluded me. You cannot understand this language. Because you belong to the other side of things. You're an inhabitant of the inside; we inhabit the outside of life.'

'I can love you like no one has ever loved a woman before,' Mouyabas said.

'What good is that, do you think? All my life is outside me now. Roaming about. Looking for me. This body that you see, this body that sleeps with you, this body of shame and sickening disgust — this is the work of a world in which my place has been killed. I have been left behind, lost — a long, long way behind myself. But you will never understand this language.'

'I'll help you,' said Mouyabas.

'You can't.'

'I . . . I could.'

'I am the body of at least twenty people. Dead and living. I am an ugly sum of mad acts, motives, and agonies of suffering.'

And Yealdara told the First Secretary her story. It took a day and a night. Mouyabas listened with ears turned to her like sunflowers.

Next morning after coffee Mouyabas went back into town.
Yealdara left the villa in the afternoon.

Things were 'sticky'. She was asked for her papers at every
corner. They were rounding people up, beating them and then
throwing them into the backs of big army lorries. Yealdara
walked the streets for a long time before calling on another of
the old man's acquaintances who lived in St James' Street. She
had cast an eye over three or four madmen walking about at
liberty, their mats under their arms. Her heart kept telling her
she would come upon Dadou sometime. But when? And where?

Old Assabrou gave her a welcome worthy of someone who
knew Amando. But it was with great sadness that he learned of
the old man's arrest. He did not even eat that evening.

'This is a sorry country,' he said over and over again. 'They
will go on killing. They will never stop. And all for nothing.'

'For peace, for there to be peace here,' Yealdara said, 'God
most be forced to go his bit of the way. All the ways are dying,
dying. . .'

'The ways, my daughter, are like men: they fall, then they get
up again. It's an ugly life we've found here, an ugly time — that
it certainly is. But there's no reason to kill hope.'

'Hope,' Yealdara echoed. 'Hope of the end, you mean?'

'No. There is no end.'

They talked at length about the country. Here the country
was often associated with God, with the dead, with everything.
The country had its flesh and its blood. There were names that
one poured like wine over the heads of things. And there was a
mingling. And it gave off hope.

'Our children, perhaps, or our children's children. Or even
our children's children's children. There is hope on every
forehead, in every eye. . .'

It was always hope, the only thing left standing here. And it
was hope, again, that led people to talk about their children's
children's children.

'My life has been lavished on all those things,' Yealdara said.

'And hope has never authorized me to look for anything more than the end.'

'Go to bed,' Assabrou said.

He pointed to a bed set up in a room adjoining what might have been called the living room. She stood up, shook hands with her host, and went and threw herself on the bed fully dressed, not even removing her shoes. Assabrou remained looking at her for a long time before going to his own bed in the room opposite.

It was a long night. Dogs barked hollowly outside. The wind blew.

It had rained all night. It was still raining when Yealdara went out to walk the streets once more. It went on drizzling until ten o'clock.

She walked and walked. It was impossible to go a hundred yards in this wretched town without meeting a madman, his mat tucked in his armpit, naked or wearing a loincloth that the wind lifted up to reveal everything. There were women, too. It was already being rumoured that these were people who had run away from all the bother of papers and partners. Legend had it that the monkeys were members of a tribe that had fled, thousands of years ago, from the taxes imposed by a ruthless government. They had asked their ancestors to intervene. To keep them from harm the ancestors had turned the entire tribe into monkeys.

For three days and nights Yealdara combed the streets and markets of the town, always showing Mouyabas's visiting-card before presenting her papers. Hunger and lack of sleep made hollows in her beautiful body. People muttered as she passed. Sometimes she heard behind her:

'What's a gorgeous creature like that doing walking in a town where cars are bought solely for trafficking in women?'

Yealdara walked on. She lost weight and it only made her

lovelier. On the made-up roads a car would pull up from time to time beside this splendid creature out walking in the hot sun, and its driver would offer to take her for a drink. Yealdara, however, walked on, ignoring these advances.

'Men are ugly — all of them, to the point where they make me sick. All except Dadou,' she thought.

Dadou had slept with her. For sex. Several times. But it had been good. It had been a solid thing. He might have ended up loving her. Her liking for nobility, her need to breathe male air — she had these from him. And everything in her said out loud: 'He is not dead. Keep walking, looking, coming, going — you'll meet up with him eventually. He is breathing.'

It was the reason why Yealdara did not give up combing the streets. She ran after every madman because of that madman of the other week who had had Dadou's face. She went everywhere her papers allowed her to. She explored in both directions the network of makers of special spirits. She found no trace of Dadou. So she decided to try to contact the Resistance.

There were three groups of 'those people' in the country: one in the centre, led by someone called Abounkira, one in the north, commanded by 'Big K', and one in the south under the orders of 'Zarathustra'. It took Yealdara three days to find out all she could about the Resistance. Thanks to her great beauty and to her papers she learned that many of the madmen roaming the town at liberty were agents of the Resistance. They walked the streets without the bother of identity checks, carrying under their arms either a bundle of clothes or the traditional sleeping-mat of the harmless wandering madman. But they were not as harmless as they looked. Old M'pene Malela, the source of most of her information about the Resistance, was another of the old man's many acquaintances. After a serious sounding-out period lasting several weeks he promised to put her in touch with the people in the jungle.

'They will kill you if you betray them.'

'I have never betrayed anyone,' Yealdara said.

'That's what they all say. But the money itch and the smell of honours triumph eventually and they end up doing the dirty on everyone.'

He introduced her to another old man, who in turn took her to the house of an old woman whom Yealdara knew from having spent four days with her once while selling old Amando's fish. For two months she was passed around among old men and women in the fish trade, being subjected to innumerable tests. Then came the crucial ceremony of affiliation.

This took place at the house of an old madwoman named Kaounsira, a martyr who had suffered the loss of her children and all her neighbours. Kaounsira lived in an old hovel on the edge of the town. On all the walls there were the sad drawings of the insane, strange pieces of equipment, and smears of excrement. The hovel comprised two rooms; an opening without a door but with a red mat for a curtain lead to the larger of the two. Yealdara, squatting on an old Nido milk tin, waited impatiently. Kaounsira moved about the room, biting her lips, scratching her partly shaven head, muttering, grumbling, cursing, singing, dancing.

'They won't be long,' she said. 'But this time is still yours, remember. If you feel you can't go on . . . you can go back. On condition you don't betray us. Once you've gone through that door, the day you decide to betray us you will die before you've opened your mouth. Here we believe very strongly. We believe in everything. Our ideas do what our bodies cannot do.'

'I shan't betray you,' Yealdara said.

'Beyond that mat,' said Kaounsira, pointing to the entrance to the second room, 'is the Resistance. And that means death.'

Two old women dressed as madwomen came in. For the first time Yealdara felt a cold fear strike at her heart. The flame of the oil lamp flickered in the draught.

'Quick — shut the door,' Kaounsira ordered.

The two newcomers shook hands with Yealdara, who was almost quaking.

'Who brings her to us?' one of them asked.

'The stem of Amando,' said Kaounsira.

'Have you had a good sniff?'

'Yes.'

'And she doesn't smell of turtle?'

'No, not of turtle.'

'What does she smell of?'

'Sheep,' said Kaounsira.

'Get ready,' the newcomer ordered Yealdara.

'Strip,' Kaounsira explained.

Yealdara stripped naked. The old woman cut the little chain that hung between her beautiful breasts.

'These things belong to the devil,' she said.

She tore off ear-rings, bracelet, watch, and rings. She anointed Yealdara's forehead with a highly perfumed grease.

'What is your name?' the old woman demanded.

'Yealdara.'

'Yealdara, you shall fight for honour, love and dignity. You shall kill because God will grant resurrection to the strong. Justice and peace shall be the sole grounds for your war. Say after me: *Kalak-Shrita.*'

'*Kalak-Shrita.*'

Yealdara repeated it after the old woman three times. She was told to kneel. She did so. The other two knelt with her, one on her left and one on her right. The old woman shaved her hair in places before covering her head with a white powder that smelled like a shroud.

'Now go in and sit down on the bench,' the old woman said, pulling the mat aside.

Yealdara went in. She would have cried out had her voice not failed her. She would have fled, but her legs failed her too. In front of her a skeleton holding a cross in what had been its right hand lay inert on a bench.

'Sit down,' the old woman insisted, 'and keep repeating "*Kalak-Shrita*".'

She sat down and said it over and over again for a long, long time. The mat fell back into place. Kaounsira began to sing a very lovely hymn. Drawn by an ineffable force, Yealdara threw herself onto her knees. The skeleton's left hand started to toll like a bell. It went on tolling for a long, long time. Then the right hand came up and traced a cross on Yealdara's forehead and another between her breasts. The two crosses dripped blood.

'Thanks be to God, thanks be to the Ancients,' said the old woman.

Yealdara collapsed and lay still. A deep silence fell. The great silence that preceded the Creation.

Next morning Yealdara came round to find Kaounsira beside her. The other two old women had left.

'I'm hungry,' Yealdara said.

Kaounsira brought her a large fish and two yams. She ate. The fish was very good.

'You'll stay here for a fortnight and then you'll return to the town. Your orders will be brought to you.'

Yealdara's whole body was covered with scabs. As she walked towards the town, a cloud of flies accompanied her. She looked in vain for the cross that the skeleton had traced on her skin. And for days she looked in vain among the many madwomen roaming the town for anyone resembling either of the two she had met at Kaounsira's house.

Time passed quickly. The scabs cleared from her legs and body and head. It was in the market one day that she came across a familiar shade.

'Dadou!' she cried.

The shade, however, took to its heels. She ran after it, but it had disappeared.

More time passed. And still more time. Yealdara slept in the market, awaiting her orders. Like all the madmen and madwomen in the town she had her mat. One day, around six in the evening, Dadou came running up to her.

'We're leaving. Tomorrow they start massacring all the insane. I'll see you again in the jungle.'

But they got no farther than old Assabrou's hut. There Dadou started telling Yealdara what his orders had required. The village. Henri and the others. The hard times. The madman's sleeping-mat. As a way of clinging to life.

'Why did you go with Mouyabas?' he asked her brusquely. 'Don't you know there are no secrets here?'

Yealdara took Dadou's hands in hers and looked at them as if she had been about to read something there. She burst into sobbing tears. Assabrou left them time to weep.

17

'Which of you wants to do something useful?' the Resistance
leader asked.

Dadou raised a finger. The Resistance leader looked at him
and smiled. In his view the man was a total derelict: he did not
even know where he came from. They had picked him up from a
heap of corpses that the soldiers had dumped in the cemetery.
Because he was still breathing, the order had gone out to pick
him up. They had picked him up. The Resistance needed
blood, and it needed able-bodied men. The blood it took from
the dying; those who could be salvaged it nursed back to health
and turned into partisans. Dadou had been nursed back to
health on those terms. But all he had done during the two years
he had been at the camp was drink and smoke. He had
contrived to manufacture some fascinating mixtures using
leaves, creepers, sap and roots. They included alcoholic drinks,
sugars, and medicines. They had earned him respect and the

title 'Dr Dadou'. Militarily, though, he was generally regarded as a non-starter. It was said that he was afraid of guns. So now everyone smiled to see him volunteering for a mission where it was a question of doing something useful. You never came back from that kind of mission. Dadou knew that.

'No, not the doctor,' said the Resistance leader. 'We'll still need our spirits here. We'll still need our strong drink.'

But Dadou insisted. 'I'll go and I'll come back. . . I'll show you that I've got blood in my veins too. . .'

'All right,' the leader said. 'Dr Dadou may come and see me in my office.'

Dadou lost no time in reporting to the Resistance leader's office. He had not had his shots that morning. His mind and body were as clear as water from a fine spring.

The leader's office was in a hut no different from the others. The interior was a picture of simplicity: a packing-case, three AK rifles, two mats and the bare earth. The earth was uneven. There was the leader's mat, and there was the visitor's mat. Dadou sat down on the visitor's mat. For a long time the leader just smiled at him.

A calabash hung from the roof of the hut. The leader stood up and reached for it. It was half full. He took a swig, then passed it to Dadou. A mark of friendship or simply a routine gesture. Dadou drank his fill, draining the calabash.

The leader could not believe his eyes. 'That was a powerful shot,' he said.

'I like it strong like that,' said Dadou.

An air of gloom settled on the leader. His face, half hidden beneath his hair and whiskers, hinted at a deep desolation.

'Don't worry on my account,' Dadou told him. 'I've lived through so many things and experienced so many situations that it seems to me I'm in the process of going beyond life. And I'm finding it tremendous fun. Anyway, if the worst comes to the worst there'll be no one to notify.'

The leader lowered his gaze. He scratched unintelligible

signs in the packed earth, cogitating at length as if faced with a decision there would be no going back on. His look gradually hardened, and his lips quivered. Suddenly his eyes went red.

'You don't want them to know? Many comrades have acted like yourself. Leaving them hope. People think you're still breathing. They tell one another: "He'll be back one morning, or one evening, or one night." They weave dreams and occasionally legends around your name. They remember your last letter.'

'It's not like that with me,' Dadou said.

The leader looked up and began to study Dadou's face. An uncomfortable feeling came over him. Had he any right to use this wretched body to bring about his revolution? In the name of what? The cause, presumably. You gave it men like the doctor. It clamoured to be stuffed sometimes with blind bodies. The cause was a carnivore, an omnivore. It could spare at least this pitiful scrap, this Dadou, who had come from no one knew where, bringing nothing.

'I have no one left in the world,' Dadou said. 'Not even myself.'

The leader's eyes went even redder. It was as if they had been dipped in fresh blood. It was as if they were about to go out from one second to the next.

'If you do not come back,' said the leader, 'I shall wear a black band around my head. But you have the right to think things over.'

'I've thought them over,' Dadou said.

The leader began to dig a little hole in the earth floor of the hut, using a dagger that he had taken from the corner where the walls of leaves and branches met. The hole clearly represented a grave. The leader tossed a piece of straw into it and filled it in.

'You will not even be entitled to that formality.'

'What does it matter?' said Dadou.

'You are going to kill someone.'

'Who?' Dadou asked.

'The First Secretary. To give our people a chance to gain a bit of ground.'

'What good will that do?' Dadou wanted to know.

The leader looked at him. These bastards who asked questions, who questioned the revolution, questioned themselves. . . Yes, maybe. But a derelict like Dr Dadou had a right to some answers.

'One doesn't ask questions of the Resistance.'

'I want to know,' Dadou said.

'There's nothing to know. We are fighting because our place is in the fight. Because they have forced us to choose between dying like insects and dying like men. We are dead men. And a dead man asks no questions. A dead man rots. Quickly or slowly, but he rots. Questions and answers are something we leave to the living. Do you know how I came to the Resistance? This bloke had his eye on my wife. He claimed I was a partisan. They tried to arrest me. I took out five soldiers and cleared off. I couldn't go back once I'd done that, once I'd killed my place back there. So I ran on, on and on. Because behind me was a void. I killed other soldiers as I went. I cut my way through their bodies. The chase lasted four days. Then I managed to get out of the town. In front of me was the jungle, and I ran into it. The trees, all the trees were like ancestors. They opened their arms to me. The birds welcomed me with their songs. For a long time I lived like an animal. I grew my hair and whiskers long. But there were my wife and my two youngsters. I thought about them. And there were my father and my mother, too, who must be mourning. I thought about them. And there were my friends. There was the church where I worshipped on Sundays. But since back there my papers were dead — the way my place was dead — I stayed here, and others joined me: Santiago and Fouty-Mak. We formed a group of leaf and grasshopper eaters. Santiago had fled the town because he had been accused of having assassinated the mayor — an accusation arising out of an old story of sexual rivalry.

Fouty-Mak had quit the town for reasons not much different from our own. The group grew. All who had lost their place back there for one reason or another came and joined us. One day we decided to go and see our wives and children. We played the papers game. But things went sour. They shot at us. We shot back. Some people got killed. We've been shooting ever since. They get killed, or maybe one of us gets killed. But we shoot without asking questions. Questions, answers — that's God's affair. You're an educated man, aren't you?'

Dadou did not reply. He was thinking about Yealdara.

'That's about how we go on: as long as we're here, we kill one another.'

Dadou told the Resistance leader his story. How from being plain Dadou he had become 'Citizen Dadou', then 'Citizen Principal', then a prisoner. He told him how he had reached this bank, this station in life.

They were still there when night fell. There had been other drinks, and they had smoked Cuban cigars.

'You can refuse to go,' the leader told him.

'No,' Dadou said. 'If I do it, this gesture will mean something. And anyway, I've always been lucky when it comes to getting out of hopeless situations.'

'I have no right to hide from you the fact that no one gets out of this sort of situation. The First Secretary is evidently in possession of some crucial facts about us. He has to die — soon. That will enable us to take a decisive step. Here's my plan. The First Secretary has an obsession: he insists on giving alms to every mad beggar who tells him he's starving. You'll get through all right. They don't arrest madmen in the town. You'll be what they call a harmless madman. The First Secretary attends St John's Cathedral every Sunday. You will ask him for something to eat. He will give you a banknote. You will pester him for another one. And that's when you will do it. His bodyguards know the boss has a weakness for mad beggars. One thing could save you: the crowd. You will dive into the crowd. They will start shooting. Lots of people will be killed. But if you dive in at the right place and take to your heels things could still go well for you. And you will go on breathing. A car will be waiting for you in the immediate vicinity of the church. If you reach it, you'll be safe. A red car. If this Sunday the First Secretary doesn't stop and listen to you, try again the next three or four Sundays. That's all — you can ask questions when you get back. Oh, I nearly forgot: all ''harmless madmen'' walk about with a mat under their arm the whole time. That's where you will conceal your gun. Leave for the town tomorrow — and good luck!'

'Good luck cannot be wished; it comes from your mother's womb,' Dadou said. 'I'm beginning to think my mother's haunches held nothing but good luck.'

'Don't boast about your mother's vagina before you've killed your man,' the leader said.

The next day Dadou left the jungle for the town, a wretched madman walking along stark naked with a mat under his arm, muttering about bottles and tobacco. Shouting and singing. There were so many of them. Walking, everlastingly walking. Fishing. All those whose lives had been messed up by papers or by some other stupidity had deliberately thrown off their clothes to take up the madman's mat and roam the streets. They had won the freedom to bawl their hearts and guts out. Psychiatrists were of the opinion that noise and overwork were adversely affecting the nerves of the people of the town and driving them insane. The man in the street tended to blame the occult practices of the white man.

Dadou idled away week after week, walking the streets of the town with his mat under his arm. He played his part well. Occasionally a group of bullying kids threw stones at him or formed a long, mocking line behind him. The bolder ones would run up and stuff something into the cleft between his buttocks. He would send them scattering without too much ill-feeling, but very soon the group would re-form for more vicious baiting. The only moments of peace came in the evenings, when Dadou spread his mat beneath the colonnades of St John's Cathedral and fell asleep with his fists clenched and his heart laid bare to the wind.

A month, two months passed. He watched for his opportunity, but his opportunity did not come. Fortunately his body was gradually becoming accustomed to this life of iron and wind, even if his devil's heart did suffer appallingly. Sundays came and went, masses came and went, but the First Secretary (had he been warned?) no longer attended. The one Sunday he did come he had to leave just before the communion. Things went on like this for three months. When he was hungry Dadou went rummaging in the dustbins of the wealthy part of town. The people at the top know how to throw things away, fortunately for the ordinary man's stomach.

On Easter Day a great crowd gathered for mass. Dadou saw the First Secretary enter the building. He followed (madmen, too, have their place in church) and went and sat on the kneeler reserved for Mouyabas and his bodyguard. The bodyguard protested, but Mouyabas calmed him: 'Let him sit there,' he murmured. For a long time Dadou's heart failed him, and he could not kill this man. But he thought of his leader's words, which he had drunk like shots of spirit. He remembered his precise, vibrant voice. His hatred. He thought of all those who were shooting in the jungle, of those who were dying, of those yet to die. At the moment of the offertory he unrolled his mat, took out his gun, and fired at point-blank range. Blood came gushing out of Mouyabas's ears.

'It was the madman,' a voice shouted. 'Stop him!'

Other voices took up the order. There was a stampede of fleeing bodies. Panic. Shouts. Commands. People swarming in all directions, some falling, some dragging children, some leaving their clothing behind. A mad throng in flight.

Dadou had forgotten about the red car. He just ran. Straight ahead. He knew, as the leader had said, that only the jungle can help those who have killed their place in the shambles and the sham. But first he must find Yealdara. And he ran through the town looking for her, knowing that soon all the town's insane would be under suspicion. All the insane throughout the land. Between eleven o'clock, when the deed was done, and one o'clock in the afternoon Dadou searched everywhere: Alafo Street, Darge Circus, the Baïkala Market, Loandji-Norte, Sakayonsa. . . No sign of her. He remembered that Yealdara often went to the tiny Yolgansa Market. He swam the river and followed Jacqo Avenue as far as Malfassi. Emerging from Yelumana Wood, Dadou saw line after line of madmen and women being taken by soldiers to Revelation Stadium. There were a couple of hundred of them. Maybe more. They were walking raggedly, heads lolling, arms behind their backs, naked and without their mats. It was possible Yealdara was among them. 'They're going to die,' Dadou thought. 'What a putrid end!'

He walked on. He still had his mat and his few rags. At Damio Square he spread his mat and fell into a heavy sleep. Flies rummaged among his rags. When night came Dadou picked up his mat and continued to Belpando-Norte. There seemed to be a strong smell of fresh blood in the air. Recalling the colour of Mouyabas's blood, Dadou wept.

At Belpando-Norte he went straight to old Assabrou's hut. Assabrou gave him an emotional welcome, hugging him like a son. They wept together.

'They're arresting all the insane,' the old man said.

'I know,' said Dadou.

'You must be hungry.'

At that moment there came a knock. They were very frightened. Nevertheless, Dadou went to open the door: it was Yealdara. She threw her arms round his neck. No one spoke, as if to do so might have killed that frail, uncertain reality.

Yealdara wept her own silent tears. Then Assabrou began to talk. About how well the fish were biting now that April was here. About the river. Yams. The fishing villages. He did not mention the murder for fear of bringing ill-luck upon his hut. As he talked he admired Dadou, who was eating a large piece of yam with an old strip of smoked lamprey. He offered him a pepper and a bit of salt, but Dadou declined. His hands were still shaking. The memory, probably. The memory of the murder.

'It's hard to eat with the hand you've used for something like that.'

'How did you do it?' Assabrou ventured to ask.

'Please — let's not talk about it.'

'They're arresting all Catholics,' Yealdara said.

'Life, in this place, is best spent guzzling fish. It's easier.'

Dadou burst out laughing. Yealdara and Assabrou looked at him in astonishment.

'To think I don't even know what the jungle hopes to get out of all this!'

'Eat,' Assabrou said. 'Our cause is just: if life ceases to be sacred, matter — all matter — will be nothing but a hollow madness.'

'I don't need ideology,' Dadou said. 'Things are jostling one another so fast in my head I wonder if I've not already gone mad in earnest. You cannot understand — I have killed because I was told: go and kill. Afterwards you feel sick. The smell of blood. Oh, mother!'

'That's war,' old Assabrou said. 'the ones who die are more fortunate than the ones who kill them. But let's talk about something else, shall we?'

'I'm tired,' Yealdara said.

They went on persecuting the insane for months. The genuine as well as the phoney. They even had the three hundred and thirteen inmates of the St Lazare Asylum shot. They also persecuted the Catholics and their masses that had devoured our late lamented First Secretary, the beloved son of the people's poverty and distress. They burned all prayer-books until the day Mouyabas appeared in a dream to the First Secretary who had replaced him, saying: 'My dear fellow, stop this nonsense. The age belongs to the people and to God.' And the dream was published in the official gazette.

BOOKS OF RELATED INTEREST

LAMENT FOR RASTAFARI
and other plays

These plays offer a dark and disturbing picture of how blacks struggle to survive in a white society and with each other.

LAMENT FOR RASTAFARI is part-ritual, part-panoramic vision of black/white relations within the confines of Rastafarian consciousness. It begins in the West Indies and follows the trials and tribulations of black families as they move from their island communities to London and finally to New York.

LIKE THEM THAT DREAM concerns the violent conflict of conscience and the need for revenge when a black orderly discovers that he is expected to look after a retired member of the white South African secret police who is dying of cancer.

THE LONG AND CHEERFUL ROAD TO SLAVERY consists of three one-act plays dealing with relationships. A Nigerian and West Indian in a London jail trying to bridge the 400 year gulf of culture and historical separation; the confrontation between an African military zealot and the ex-minister of the corrupt ousted African government; and the marital tangles between a wealthy West Indian who has chosen a life of poverty in Britain and his elitist wife who fails to understand his voluntary exile from their narrow society at home.

Edgar White was born in the West Indies. He has lived in the United States and England. His plays have been successfully presented in New York, London and in Africa.

by
EDGAR WHITE

Redemption Song
and other plays

Edgar White

REDEMPTION SONG, THE BOOT DANCE, LES FEMMES NOIRES

These plays by West Indian playwright Edgar White explore the themes of exile, submission and defiance as reflected in black experience.

REDEMPTION SONG is a powerful blend of melodrama and ritual. A poet, Legion Bramble, returns to his island homeland during the Mummers' Festival after an unhappy stay in Britain, to reclaim his West Indian identity.

THE BOOT DANCE, set in an English mental hospital, traces the relationships between Lazarus Mphele, an exiled South African dancer, a cynical West Indian guard named Gibbs, and Janette, a mixed-race teenager who once tried to murder her violent father.

LES FEMMES NOIRES probes the lives of black women in New York A presence in the play - almost a character in its own right - is the omnipresent TV screen, purveyor of cultural values and commodities, which both beckons and excludes those in its sway.

Edgar White was born in Montserrat, West Indies. Five of his plays have been produced by Joseph Papp's New York Shakespeare Theatre. REDEMPTION SONG was premiered at Riverside Studios, London, and THE BOOT DANCE at the Tricycle Theatre, London. His plays are being performed world-wide.

THE RISING

A Novel by

EDGAR WHITE

Born into a rich house boasting money, cars and servants, and whose matriarch, Mother Frances, rules with a rod of iron, Desmie is a passionate and sensual young woman. She has every luxury that her mother's vast wealth can provide, but is denied that luxury most coveted by the young; freedom. For some time it appears that Mother Frances has succeeded in bullying her daughter into submission, but Desmie rebels when she meets and falls for the island's most glamorous gambler and womanizer. Their affair, as steamy as the Caribbean island on which it takes place, is Desmie's downfall: ostracized by society, shamed in the eyes of her family, dominated by her mother once more, her life is over before it has barely begun.

Edgar White brings to this ferocious drama of passion and guilt the poetry of an exceptional and experienced playwright (*Lament for Rastafari* and *Redemption Song*). He reveals the secrets of an island life with its own power structure and its own etiquette. An island whose inhabitants are bound by a code so rigid and inappropriate as to be unenforceable – a code which is forever flaunted and violated.

Jelly Roll Morton's Last Night at the Jungle Inn

an imaginary memoir
Samuel Charters

Whether or not he is the orginator of jazz and blues'—as he claimed when refuting Ripley's attribution of this title to WC Handy on a 'Believe It or Not' radio program in the late Thirties— Ferdinand 'Jelly Roll' Morton was certainly the jazz musician without a peer. Like the setting of this Imaginary Memoir, the Jungle Inn, itself always changing its name, Morton's life, as he recounted and constantly embellished it, was a swaggering 'work in progress'. No one to this day has been able to sift the fact from fiction. The author accurately catches the breezy tone of Morton's recorded narrative and expands throw-away biographical hints into a kind of Morton apocrypha which will be reveled in by all the master's afficionados.

SAMUEL CHARTERS

THE ROOTS OF THE BLUES

'I went to Africa to find the roots of the blues'. It was with this intention that Samuel Charters, the blues and jazz expert and author of *The Legacy of the Blues,* journeyed through West Africa, trying to uncover the origins of a music which had a profound impact on the art, music, culture and politics of the West and in particular in the United States. What began as a genealogical study of how the blues was handed down from the African slaves to musicians of today via the slave ships, the farms and the urban ghetto became something much more complex.

In Africa, Samuel Charters discovered a music which was not just a part of the past but a very vital living part of African culture. This book details and analyzes the meeting between a Westerner and a thriving culture new to him. It reveals Charters' remarkable analytical talent in discussing African folk music and its relationship with American blues and demonstrates his power as a descriptive writer. It is a musical exploration and at the same time a travelogue of the Africa he uncovered: markets, villages, the heat and dust and the road. The author also draws on the accounts of earlier explorers. His extensive quotations of lyrics from songs and wonderful photographs of the musicians make this a unique contribution to our understanding of a culture and its music.

Mr. Jabi and Mr. Smythe

a novel

samuel · charters

Set in a new African state in the late
seventies, this tersely written and fast-
moving novel concerns the return, after
a ten-year absence, of Tony Smythe, a
white British ex-commissioner, to the
area he once administered. He stays
with his old African friend and
colleague, Mr. Jabi, a retired school
teacher, and his wife in their village
compound. Smythe's return is
motivated by his rootless existence in
Great Britain after Independence forced
him into retirement, by his wife's death,
and he is also troubled by questions
concerning his past role as an
"imperialist" in Africa.

Set against the colorful, busy and noisy
life of an African village compound, this
novel begins by exploring the moral
issues surrounding post-Imperial involvement in African development. However,
beneath this there is the much broader
theme of wasted idealism — of commit-
ment, and of the meaning of loyalty to
an idea.